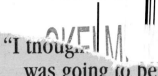

"I thought... was going to be my job."

He swung his gaze to meet hers. He was certain that he'd heard wrong. "Ma'am?"

She held his gaze, though he sensed she was nervous. Still she pulled back her shoulders. "I mean, since I am going to be your wife, it only seems right that the children stay with us."

For a moment his head swam as if a prizefighter had landed a knockout punch. "My what?"

Mrs. Clements stepped forward, wearing a broad grin that hinted at trouble. "Miss Smyth *is* the bit of news I was referring to."

Matthias's head started to throb. The last thing he needed was a riddle. "What the devil are you talking about, Mrs. Clements?"

The older woman smoothed her hands over her white apron and cleared her throat. "We ordered you a wife. Miss Smyth is your *fiancée*."

* * *

The Unexpected Wife
Harlequin Historical #708—June 2004

Acclaim for MARY BURTON'S
recent works

Rafferty's Bride

"Ms. Burton has written a romance filled with passion
and compassion, forgiveness and humor; the kind of
well-written story that truly touches the heart
because you can empathize with the characters."
—*Romantic Times*

The Perfect Wife

"Mary Burton presents an intricate theme that questions if
security rather than attraction defines the basis of love."
—*Romantic Times*

The Colorado Bride

"A heart-touching romance about love, loss
and the realities of family. In her finely crafted historical,
Mary Burton manages to vibrate some sensitive
and intense modern issues."
—*Romantic Times*

"This talented writer is a virtuoso, who strums the hearts
of readers and composes an emotional tale.
I was spellbound."
—*Rendezvous*

MARY BURTON

The Unexpected Wife

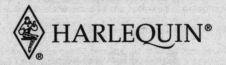

HARLEQUIN®

TORONTO • NEW YORK • LONDON
AMSTERDAM • PARIS • SYDNEY • HAMBURG
STOCKHOLM • ATHENS • TOKYO • MILAN • MADRID
PRAGUE • WARSAW • BUDAPEST • AUCKLAND

105267110

ISBN 0-373-29308-9

THE UNEXPECTED WIFE

www.eHarlequin.com

Printed in U.S.A.

Available from Harlequin Historicals and
MARY BURTON

A Bride for McCain #502
The Colorado Bride #570
The Perfect Wife #614
Christmas Gold #627
"Until Christmas"
Rafferty's Bride #632
The Lightkeeper's Woman #693
The Unexpected Wife #708

Please address questions and book requests to:
Harlequin Reader Service
U.S.: 3010 Walden Ave., P.O. Box 1325, Buffalo, NY 14269
Canadian: P.O. Box 609, Fort Erie, Ont. L2A 5X3

For Mike and Nancy,
the Montana cowboy and his Portuguese bride

Prologue

Crickhollow, Montana
May, 1879

Hilda Marie Clements held open the door to her mercantile, as two men with low crowned hats and upturned collars filed through. Each carried a lantern, but the meager lights did little to chase away the predawn shadows that stretched across the assortment of boxes, barrels and crates. A chill clung to the early morning air, a reminder that even though June was but weeks away, winter had not fully released its cruel grip.

Mrs. Clements moved toward her counter as her visitors took seats on twin barrels nearby.

Closest to her was Holden McGowan. His long lean body, draped in buckskin, was well muscled by years of driving a stagecoach team. Nearing his thirty-fifth year, Holden had been in the valley for seven years. A trapper first and later a miner, he'd moved into town three years ago to open the Starlight stage line.

Next to Holden sat Frank Trotter. He'd moved to the valley eighteen months ago to help his daughter, Elise, and his son-in-law Matthias when Elise had become ill during her third pregnancy. Elise and her stillborn child had died six days after Frank had arrived. Trotter's graying beard and hollow eyes testified to the sorrow he'd endured since he'd buried his wife and then his only child. He'd aged fifteen years in the last two years.

Mrs. Clements was impatient to get the meeting started. Her husband, Seth, would wake soon and she wasn't interested in a lecture on meddling. "I know Frank ain't got much time. He's got to get on the trail at first light so he can get back to the ranch in time for lunch. So let's get to business."

Frank nodded, silent and grim. Of the three, he looked the most uneasy, the most worried.

Holden swung his gaze to Mrs. Clements. The plump Virginian had agreed to handle all their correspondence. "You said she wrote us another letter."

Mrs. Clements pushed back a stray wisp of hair

before she dug pudgy fingers into the deep pockets of her apron and pulled out a wrinkled envelope. ''She sure did.''

Holden leaned forward a fraction, nervously tapping his long fingers on his thigh. ''So did she accept our marriage proposal?''

Mrs. Clements grinned. ''She's ready and willing to travel to Crickhollow on our instruction.'' She shifted in her seat with excitement. ''And she has sent along a tintype for us to look at. Now she's warned us that it's a couple of years old, but she says it's still very accurate.''

Holden's gaze brightened as he held out his hand to Mrs. Clements. ''A woman who thinks about the details. I like that.''

Mrs. Clements hesitated before she handed Holden the picture. ''She's not a real beauty,'' she said, passing the picture to the coachman as he moved closer. ''But she looks sturdy—good hearty peasant stock as my mother used to say. Looks like she'd weather many a winter here.''

Holden tilted the picture closer to the lantern light as he studied it. Frank stayed seated, nervously tapping his knee with his hand.

The coachman's eyebrows knotted as he studied the tintype. A small oval face, slightly pointed chin, and peaches-and-cream complexion. A simple hat obscured most of her hair, but her unsmiling lips were full and her pale eyes filled with a softness that made her approachable. She wore a dark gray dress with a high collar. No hint of lace adorned the simple dress. "She looks a bit severe."

Mrs. Clements waved away his concern. "I never put too much stock in pictures. Those big city photographers make you sit still for so long your muscles cramp. No one's interested in smiling by the time the flash explodes."

"I've never had my picture taken, so I'll take your word for it. How old did you say she was again?" Holden handed the picture to Frank.

Frank shifted on his barrel, uncomfortable. He glanced at the image. "Sure hope she ain't as rigid as she looks."

"She's not rigid," Mrs. Clements said, defending her choice of the original six applicants to their mail-order bride ad in the *San Francisco Morning Chronicle*. Abigail Smyth had the neatest handwriting and her letters had been full of rich details. She spoke of dreams, new beginnings and making a home for them. "We've all read her letters. They're lovely, full of wonderful ideas and plans. I can tell she has a fine heart."

Frank scrutinized the picture, and then released

a sigh. "Looking at her face makes this all so real. I never thought it would get this far."

Impatient, Mrs. Clements rubbed her thigh. "Frank, you're the one that came to us with the idea of finding your son-in-law a wife in the first place."

Frank nodded wearily. "I know. I promised Elise I'd find someone to care for Matthias and the boys."

"So what's your problem?" Mrs. Clements said.

Frank rubbed his bloodshot eyes. "*Talking* about finding a wife for Matthias and actually *getting* a wife is worlds apart. He's not a man to cross."

Holden stretched out his long legs as if to get comfortable. "I got to admit, I'm a little nervous about this myself. I don't want to be around when he finds out what we've been up to."

Mrs. Clements bit back her growing impatience with Frank. *Men.* They didn't have the stomach for the hard work. "Holden, now you aren't waffling on me, are you?"

He sat straighter. "Nope. I am committed to this. What's her name again?"

"Abigail Smyth," Mrs. Clements supplied.

"Matthias is going to be furious," Frank said.

"There's no way Matthias can handle his home-stead and take care of the young ones," Mrs. Clements added. "They need a mother. He needs a wife."

"And we *need* Matthias to stay in the valley," Holden said. "He's a damn good man who loves this land. He's also a crack shot who's not afraid to deal with renegades and outlaws, both of which we don't need especially now that the railroad is scouting a rail line this way."

Mrs. Clements nodded. "This community is just starting to thrive and we can't afford to lose ground now."

Frank rose and walked to the window. The morning sun's orange-and-red lights simmered below the horizon. "I ain't so sure if he'll ever love another woman."

"This ain't about *love*, Frank," Mrs. Clements said. "It's about *marriage*. The two don't have much to do with each other in Montana."

Frank nervously tugged at the cuffs of his jacket. "And what are we gonna do if Matthias digs his heels in? What if he tells this Abigail to go on back to San Francisco?"

"We won't allow it," Mrs. Clements said. Steel coated each word.

Frank tightened his long fingers around the rim of his weathered felt hat. "All this lying just don't set well with me."

Mrs. Clements waved away his concern. "I have faith that the two of them will work this out."

Despite her words, she said a silent prayer that they had done the right thing. Matthias was a man of few words, and he was friendly enough. Sure, his ice-blue eyes burned like Satan's when he was angry, but he never threw the first punch or stirred up trouble. A soldier, bounty hunter and most recently a rancher, there wasn't a better man to call if you were in trouble. When Matthias Barrington gave his word, he moved heaven and earth to keep it.

Still, crossing Matthias Barrington was about as smart as tangling with a rattler or a grizzly. "Matthias will be glad in the end."

Holden rolled his eyes heavenward. "If he don't kill us all first."

Chapter One

"Abby, quick, grab the muffins!" Cora O'Neil shouted from across the basement kitchen. The heavyset Irish woman punched her meaty fist into a mound of leavened bread dough. "By the smell of them they're about to burn."

Abby set down the bag of flour on the wide kitchen table and, wiping her hands on her apron, hurried to the large cast-iron stove. Using her apron as a mitt, she opened the heavy door and pulled out the tin. The heat of the hot metal quickly burned through the thin cotton fabric and scorched her fingers. She dropped the pan on top of the stove with a loud *whack*.

"Hurry up, now," Cora said. "Fill that basket on the tray with the muffins while they're still hot. You know how your Uncle Stewart gets when 'is muffins is cold."

Abby pushed a sweaty strand of hair off her face. She'd been anxious to get her chores done early today so that she could intercept the postman before he dropped off the morning mail and Uncle Stewart read it. She checked the heart-shaped watch pinned to her blouse. Nine-fifteen. She'd have to hurry.

She dropped the hot muffins into the basket lined with linen. She'd been corresponding with a man in Montana for months now. In his last letter, he'd asked for her hand in marriage. In her last letter, she'd accepted. Now all that remained was the final travel details. Her hands trembled with excitement as she tried to picture her new life, her fresh start.

Since her parents' deaths and her move to her uncle's house in California ten years ago, she'd been an unwanted annoyance to her relatives. Because they'd been unwilling to sponsor her in society, she'd soon found herself trapped between the world of the people who lived upstairs and those who lived downstairs.

Eight years ago, she'd fallen in love with a young lawyer she'd met through her uncle. His name had been Douglas Edmondson. Blessed with blond hair and blue eyes, he had a poet's heart and a gift for words that made her knees go week. She'd fallen in love almost immediately.

Words of love tripped easily from Douglas's

tongue, but love had not been what he was after. A night's romp in the gardens had been his only desire. Abby learned of his shallow heart too late and in the end he'd made a fool out of her.

Her uncle had been furious about the scandal, but he'd not thrown her out. As an unspoken payment, she'd retreated to her kitchens and taken her place with the servants.

In January, when her cousin Joanne announced her engagement, Abby suddenly realized life was passing her by. Her years of hiding ended. She wanted a fresh start, a new beginning.

So, she'd taken action. She'd answered the ad in the *San Francisco Morning Chronicle* for a mail-order bride and taken her life into her own hands.

Abby shoved aside the memory and hurried up the stairs. Several deep, even breaths erased the tightness in her chest.

A year from now she'd be married, living a new fresh life filled with possibilities. In Montana she'd not be trapped between social circles, and perhaps, God willing, she'd be cradling her own babe in her arms.

"Stop your daydreaming!" Cora shouted.

Abby straightened. "Sorry, Cora."

Her dreams were within her grasp, but she'd have to move carefully. Uncle Stewart would stop her if he knew her intentions. His society friends would frown upon him if word got out his ward, who'd already disgraced him once, had become a mail-order bride.

So far she'd managed to keep the letters a secret. Normally, Uncle Stewart read the mail in the evening, so it had been easy for her to sift through the letters unnoticed. However, today her uncle had taken a day off from work in preparation for her cousin's engagement party, which was to be held in two days. He'd chosen to sleep late and was having his breakfast an hour later. The entire household, which worked around his schedule, was in a tizzy over the change.

As she reached the top step, she nudged open the door that led to the dining room with her foot.

Her Aunt Gertrude, Uncle Stewart and cousin Joanne sat at the large finely polished dining table. Her uncle, as he did each day, was reading the *Chronicle*, while her aunt and cousin chatted about her cousin's upcoming wedding. None turned to greet her as she entered the room.

Abby set her tray on the side table. She glanced nervously through the double doors of the dining room toward the front door. The post always arrived at nine twenty. If she hurried, she'd make it.

Managing a smile, she placed the coffee cups in

front of her uncle first, then her aunt and her cousin last. As she filled each cup and placed the muffins on the table, Stewart reached for the strawberry jam on the table and started to spread it on his muffin.

Wiping her hands on her brown skirt, she moved toward the door that led to the foyer, grateful for the first time that they'd not acknowledged her.

As she reached the threshold, her uncle set down his knife on his white porcelain plate. "Abigail, a letter arrived for you yesterday."

The nerves in her body tightened and she could feel the blood draining from her face. Slowly she faced her uncle. "I got the post yesterday. There was no letter for me."

"The postman held it back. He thought it odd that you've been receiving so much mail lately." He bit into the muffin and carefully set it back on the plate.

"If it's my letter, then I'd like to have it," she said, careful to keep her voice calm.

"Who is Matthias Barrington?" he said.

Abby felt the color drain from her face.

Aunt Gertrude's eyes darkened with suspicion. "I don't know any Barringtons in San Francisco."

"He's not from San Francisco," Stewart said. "He's from Montana."

Gertrude poured cream in her tea. "Good Lord,

Montana? I wasn't sure if anyone really lived there, let alone anyone who could write.''

Abby crushed back the welling panic. ''You opened my letter.''

''I did,'' said her uncle. ''And why shouldn't I? This is my house and everything that happens in it is my business. ''Now answer my question. Who is Matthias Barrington?''

She'd known this day would come. She'd rehearsed what she would say to her aunt and uncle a thousand times, but the words suddenly caught in her throat.

Joanne lifted her gaze from several trousseau sketches she was examining. Golden curls framed a heart-shaped face and emphasized pale skin and lavender eyes. The blue watered silk morning wrapper hugged her delicate figure to perfection. ''Cat got your tongue?'' she purred.

Abby stared at her cousin. Stewart and Gertrude had always thought their daughter perfect, especially in comparison to a niece who'd never been exposed to the finer social graces.

Abby managed a slight shrug of her shoulders. ''He is a rancher in Montana.''

''And what business does he have with you?'' Gertrude said.

A gold signet ring on Stewart's right pinky finger

winked in the morning light as he pulled the letter from his pocket. He laid it by his plate. "It seems this Barrington fellow is talking some nonsense about marriage to our Abigail."

"Marriage!" Joanne laughed. "I thought you'd given up on love after Douglas made a fool out of you."

Abby drew in a steadying breath, determined not to show her anger.

Annoyed, Gertrude tapped her finger against the linen tablecloth. "You told me nothing of this."

Abby held out her hand. "May I have my letter?"

Stewart buttered his muffin. "Not until you tell us what this is all about. How could you even come to know such a man?"

Oddly, instead of fear she felt relieved to have it all in the open. "I answered his ad in the _Chronicle_ for a mail order bride."

Gertrude's cup clattered down hard against its saucer. Stewart's thin face whitened. "Why would you embarrass us in such a way? Haven't we done right by you these last ten years? Lord knows we stood by you when we should have tossed you into the street."

His words nearly rekindled the guilt that had kept

her in check for so many years. "This has nothing to do with you."

"Don't be ridiculous," he snapped. "Everything you do is my concern. When it's time for you to marry, I will see that you marry a suitable man."

"When I marry?" For a moment anger tightened her throat. How many times had she heard this? "If I stay in San Francisco, I will never marry. Dearest Joanne and her gossip have seen to that. And I want a family of my own. It is time for me to move on."

Joanne tossed her napkin on the table. "This is all very fascinating, but Mother, we're going to be late to the dressmakers, if we delay too long."

Aunt Gertrude nodded. "In a minute, dear." She lifted her sharp gaze to Abby. "If it's a husband you want, I'm sure we can find one. In fact, I heard the butcher, Joshua Piper, is looking for another wife. He seems rather fond of you."

At forty-seven, the butcher had four unruly sons and a mother who still lived with him. It struck Abby then that on her last visit to his shop he'd spent extra time with her. It also explained the extra lamb chop in her order. "I want a fresh start," she said. "Away from the city."

Stewart pinched the bridge of his nose. "The city is far better than Montana. I've heard tales about that wretched land. It's full of cutthroats and murderers.''

Abby could feel the tension building in the muscles at the base of her back. "It's my choice."

"You can't marry without my permission," Stewart said.

"I am five and twenty, Uncle, and well able to take care of myself. I no longer need your permission."

His face reddened and his lips flattened into a grim line. "Since when did you get so independent?"

Joanne rose. "Father, I really don't care if she stays or goes. As long as she's here to cook for my wedding reception. Freddie's parents do love her scones and teacakes."

Stewart didn't take his gaze off Abby. "Your cousin is not going anywhere."

"I am," Abby said, firmly now.

"How do you propose to pay for this trip east?" he said.

"Mr. Barrington said in his last letter that he was going to send me money."

"He sent twenty-five dollars. And I pocketed it."

For a moment her head spun. "You can't do that, it's mine!"

He stuck out his fleshy chin. "I can do anything I please in my house."

Enraged, Abby snatched up the letter off the table. "You've no right to that money."

He rose to his feet. "I've every right, young lady. And you will not talk any more about this farce of a marriage to a stranger. I will not have people in this town talking about me and whispering about another of your scandalous deeds."

Aunt Gertrude pursed her lips together. "I think perhaps a marriage to the butcher is not such a bad idea. In fact, I will talk to his mother today." She rose. "As soon as Joanne is safely wed, we will see to Abigail. It's become quite clear to me that she doesn't appreciate what we've done for her and it's time she leaves."

"I believe you are right, my dear," Stewart said. "The matter is settled. Abigail will marry the butcher as soon as it can be arranged."

Abby's stomach curdled. "I'm not marrying the butcher. I am marrying Mr. Barrington."

"Abigail," Stewart said. "Don't you have work to do in the kitchen?"

Clutching Mr. Barrington's letter in her hand, she glared at her uncle. "You can't dismiss me like this!"

Gertrude and Joanne stared at Abby in shocked silence.

''Return to the kitchens. I've my breakfast to finish.'' He shifted his attention back to his paper.

Frustrated, Abby rushed out of the room. Instead of going to the kitchens she ran up the center staircase to her third-floor room. Breathless, she slammed the door to her room and sat down on her bed. Sweat beaded on her forehead as her heart pounded her ribs.

Minutes passed before she remembered the letter clutched in her hand. Slowly, she uncurled her clenched fingers and smoothed out the envelope.

Her frustration faded as she looked at the familiar handwriting. Lifting the letter to her nose, she inhaled the scents of wood smoke. She closed her eyes as she had done a hundred times before and tried to picture Matthias Barrington.

For reasons she could not explain, she pictured an older man, with weathered features and kind eyes that hinted at his loneliness. She imagined their marriage would be founded on friendship, hard work and the desire to build a life together.

Calmer, Abby pulled out the letter and unfolded it.

Miss Smyth, I am so pleased you've accepted my marriage offer. You will be a welcome addition to our little valley and everyone is quite excited to meet you. I have enclosed twenty-five dollars for your travel expenses. I spoke with the gentleman who runs the stage line into Crickhollow, a Mr. Holden McGowan, and he assures me that at this time of year, you should have nothing but a safe and pleasant journey. I count the days until you arrive.

M. Barrington.

Abby carefully folded the letter and replaced it in the envelope. She moved to the small chest at the foot of her bed that contained everything that belonged to her—a faded tintype of her parents, a small mirror that had been her mother's, her grandmother's tablecloth, two dresses and the neatly bound stack of letters Mr. Barrington had written her.

She drew in a steadying breath. "By month's end, Mr. Barrington."

At midnight, only a small gaslight sconce flickered in the hallway as Abby slipped down the back staircase. Careful not to make a sound, she clutched her belongings, now bundled in her grandmother's white linen tablecloth. The house was quiet.

Gingerly, Abby set down her bundle by the door and tiptoed into her uncle's study. She'd long ago learned from one of the servants where he kept his money. Her uncle always thought himself clever with his secret hiding places but there was little the servants didn't know or discuss about their employers.

Lighting a wall gas lamp, she moved across the thick-carpeted floor to his bookcase. She found the richly bound copy of Shakespeare's *Twelfth Night* and opened it. Carefully, she counted out twenty-five crisp dollars and tucked them in her reticule.

Quietly replacing the book she moved across the room and turned the gaslight off. She picked up her bundle and opened the study door, wincing when it squeaked unexpectedly.

Abby swallowed her fear and hurried down the back hallway, her heart thundering in her chest.

Like it or not, after tonight, there would be no coming home.

She was committed to Montana and Mr. Barrington.

Chapter Two

Every muscle in Abby's body ached.

She'd been in the stagecoach for nearly twelve hours and was certain that if the wheels hit another rut or the wagon was forced to detour around another swollen river, or her traveling companion, Mr. Stokes, began snoring again, she'd scream.

The wagon came to an abrupt halt, and she toppled forward into the oversize lap of Mr. Stokes. He started awake and wiped the spittle from his mouth, staring down at her. He smiled. "Madam."

Mr. Craig Stokes had been riding with her for the last ten hours. A scout for the railroad, Mr. Stokes chatted endlessly about his job. Dirt grayed his black wool suit and his cuffs and collar had long ago turned brown. Flecks of food still nested in his mustache and he smelled of sausages and sweat.

When he was not snoring in his sleep, he was staring at her.

Abby scrambled off his lap and retreated to her corner of the coach. "Excuse me. I lost my balance."

"Any time." He tugged his vest down over his ample belly. "It's beyond me why a woman of quality like yourself would be traveling alone in these parts. It's rough county, miss, and no place for a woman."

Abby had asked herself that same question a half-dozen times over the last couple of days. Living in her aunt and uncle's San Francisco house, she felt her life had become an endless stream of work, but there she understood the predictable pattern. Here everything was unknown, including the man she'd intended to marry.

"I assure you, I am fine."

Mr. Stokes shrugged. "If you insist." Suddenly restless now, he banged on top of the carriage. "What is it this time, man?"

"A rider up ahead and a wagon with a broken wheel," the driver shouted back.

Abby pushed back the carriage window drape and poked her head out to get a better look.

Twenty yards ahead, she saw an old man sitting on the side of the road next to a wagon. Two small young boys, their dirty faces peeking out from their floppy hats, squatted beside him, jabbing sticks in the mud. The wagon tilted to the right, the wheel burrowed deeply in the thick mud. The team of horses, two fine-looking chestnut mares, had been unhitched from the wagon and were grazing beside the road.

Her heart melted when she saw the two young boys. She raised her hand to wave when she spotted another man standing next to the wagon. Her appraisal took only seconds but it was enough to know the man was angry. The scowl on his raw-boned face had her lowering her hand and retreating back a fraction.

The stranger glanced up toward the coach, his eyes narrowing. He started to walk toward them, moving with the grace and power of a wild animal. He was tall, with broad well-muscled shoulders that made her think of the bare-knuckled boxers she'd seen at a carnival years ago.

Utterly masculine. A hint of warmth had her blushing. Abby was surprised by her reaction. Passion was the last thing she needed or wanted.

Still, she looked deeper beneath his black Stetson and studied his dark hair tied back at the nape of his neck with a piece of rawhide. His hair accentuated his chiseled features, and the uncompromising hardness of a jaw covered in dark stubble. His range coat flapped open as he moved, revealing muddied work pants and a dark blue shirt and scuffed boots that stretched to his knees.

Whoever this man was, he was dangerous.

Matthias Barrington was in a foul mood.

He nodded back to his father-in-law Frank and his sons. "I'll be right back. Keep an eye on the boys. I need to talk to Holden."

Frank stood, tapping his bony fingers against his thigh. "Looks like he's got a woman aboard."

"I don't care." He strode toward the stagecoach.

The day had started going sour from the minute he'd risen. Not only did his wagon have a broken wheel, but his father-in-law had announced this morning that he was leaving Crickhollow and heading back to Missouri. Matthias knew the old man wasn't happy and that this past winter had been hard on him, but he'd thought Frank would stay at least the summer.

Without Frank to watch over the boys, he was in trouble. Matthias didn't dare dwell on how far behind schedule he was already this early in the season.

Matthias glanced up toward the stagecoach driver, Holden McGowan, and extended his hand.

He'd known Holden since Matthias and his late wife had arrived in the valley five years ago. The man always had a quick smile and a joke to share. But today when he looked at Matthias, his expression was tight, nervous even.

"Everything all right?" Matthias said.

Holden nodded, as if recovering from the shock of seeing him. "Right as rain. I just wasn't expecting to see you here. Looks like you hit a bit of trouble, though."

Frank came up behind Matthias. "Our wagon hit a rut and broke a wheel."

Holden glanced quickly at Frank. "Shame."

Matthias pulled off his hat and wiped the sweat from his brow. "You got room to take Frank and the children into town? I'll fix the wagon and follow behind you in the next hour or two."

Holden shifted in his seat. "Oh sure, will do."

Matthias nodded. "Thanks."

He glanced up and saw a woman staring at him. She had wide green eyes that testified to just how naive she was. Her cheeks turned pink when their gazes locked and she retreated back into the coach.

He swore under his breath.

Crickhollow was a barren, isolated town where few women ventured. If this Society Miss, with her wide-eyed expression, pale skin and fancy hat, had half a brain, she'd run from this wild territory, which chewed up nearly every woman that tried to call it home.

He strode back to the buckboard where his sons played. If Montana was going to be tamed, it needed women who knew how to work—not genteel ladies like Society Miss.

He glanced down at his boys, wondering what he was going to do with them now that Frank was leaving. At three and four, they were too young to leave alone at the cabin or take out on the range with him each day.

There was Mrs. Clements. She'd taken in the boys the first couple of weeks after Elise had died. He and Frank were so torn up with sorrow they weren't able to properly care for the boys.

Mrs. Clements had done right by the boys but farming them out stuck in Matthias's craw. He liked having his children close. But with so much work to be done he didn't know what else to do.

When Matthias reached the wagon, his youngest, three-year-old Tommy, held out his hands and started to cry. Instinctively, he reached out and lifted the boy. The child laid his head on his father's shoulder.

Tommy hated riding in wagons. They upset his

stomach. Matthias glanced at his oldest boy's dirty face. Four-year-old Quinn grinned up at him.

"Pa, do we get to ride in the coach?"

Matthias shoved out a sigh. "Sure do."

Frank came up behind him. "We don't mind waiting with you here while you fix the wagon."

Matthias glared at Frank. "I'd rather the boys get into town so Mrs. Clements can give them a hot meal."

"I got hard tack in the pack. We don't mind helping you."

"I want the boys in town by dark."

"But…"

"No buts." Irritation gave each word extra bite.

Frank's sudden desire to stay behind puzzled him. The man was hell-bent on leaving, and Matthias had spent the better part of the morning arguing with Frank about his decision to leave. Later, pride had kept him from asking Frank to stay again, but seeing the boys now made him rethink a lot of things in his life. "Frank, any way you can postpone this trip East? Just a couple of months."

Frank glanced toward the stagecoach. "Time I got on with my life."

Matthias bit back the oath that sprang to mind. Frank's leaving had put him in a predicament. "Get on the stage with the boys. When I've fixed the wheel, I'll follow."

Frank picked up his bag. "Sure."

Matthias took Quinn in his arms. The boys clung to his neck as he walked the twenty yards to the stage.

He nodded to Holden. "Again, I'm obliged."

"Think nothing of it." Nervous, Holden tightened the reins around his gloved hand. "There's only room enough for the boys inside. Frank, you'll have to ride up top with me."

Frank glanced toward the coach's interior as if he were worried. "Fine."

Matthias set Quinn down so that he could reach for the door handle. The boy fussed and clung to his leg. Inwardly Matthias sighed. The boys, who both shared their mother's blond hair and deep blue eyes, had been clingy and restless since Elise had died last year. He'd hoped time would take care of that, but lately the boys seemed more fretful than ever. Last night they'd been so restless he'd pulled them in bed with him. That had been a mistake. Quinn had ended up sleeping sideways in the bed, poking him in the ribs with his feet most of the night. While Tommy had snored so loud that Matthias would have sworn he was sleeping with a three-hundred-pound cowhand.

With a boy in each arm, Matthias strode to the wagon door. Society Miss, with her perky nose and fussy clothes stared at him. He could only imagine her thoughts. He looked rougher than a dried prairie and the boys looked just as bad.

But as they got closer, she didn't cower, but studied him with sharp intelligent eyes that didn't seem to miss a detail.

Her gaze shifted to the boys, who he had to admit smelled bad. Miss Society's eyes softened when she looked at Tommy and Quinn. She pitied them, he reckoned. They looked wild and untamed as if wolves had raised them.

Pride had him straightening his shoulders. Elise had always kept the boys scrubbed clean, but since she'd died he'd not had the time to fuss over them.

Guilt ate at his gut. Lately, he did everything half-ass. Even with Frank's help there was never enough time to do anything right. Before Elise had gotten sick it had been a struggle to keep up, but lately he was fighting a losing battle.

If he hadn't loved this land so much, he'd have left when Elise died. But with only three months before he owned his land free and clear, he hated to quit. If he could hold on, he'd have a legacy for his boys that they would be proud of.

Matthias reached for the stagecoach door handle.

Frank pushed past him and grabbed it first. "I'll settle the boys inside. You get back to the wagon."

Tommy started to fuss and cling to Matthias tighter. "I want Pa."

Matthias held on to the boy. "I'll settle the children."

Matthias opened the door and was surprised to see that Society Miss was not alone. A large man wearing a dusty black suit glared at him. Society Miss's wide-eyed expression had given him the impression that she wasn't married. Of course, it only made sense that she was and that this man was likely her husband. Only a half-witted woman would travel to Montana alone.

More irritated than before, he met the man's gaze. "My boys will be riding with you as far as Crickhollow."

The man puffed out his chest and tugged his vest down.

"I paid for my seat," the man said through tight lips. "And I've no intention of sharing it with a couple of dirty children."

Matthias yearned to toss the man on the side of the road, but before he could respond, Society Miss scooted over in her seat to make more room.

"They may sit with me," she said. "There's plenty of room on my seat."

Matthias lifted his gaze to the woman and for the first time looked past the yards of fabric and the netting of her hat that covered her face. Her hair was blond and it curled at the ends as if the stands strained against the pins that held it in a tight chignon.

Her face was all angles, plain by most standards, and nothing like Elise's soft, round features. But Society Miss's vivid green eyes brought an energy to her that made her anything but nondescript.

His gaze skimmed to her full lips. For just an instant, he wondered what they tasted like. His reaction was not only unexpected, but unwanted, as well. He chalked it up to too many lonely nights.

"I'm obliged, miss," Matthias said.

"Abigail Smyth," she supplied.

Suddenly, Holden coughed. "Best get a move on, I have a schedule to keep."

Matthias's eyes narrowed against the sun's glare. Holden was right. Time was wasting.

He lifted Quinn and set him in the coach. The boy turned to him as if he'd bolt when Society Miss said softly, "I promise I don't bite."

The boy clung to his father.

"Let loose, boy," Matthias said.

"I've a mirror in my reticule," Society Miss offered. "Would you like to see it?"

Tommy never passed on a gadget. He turned and stared at her.

She reached in her purse and pulled out a small oval mirror in a mother-of-pearl case. The mirror reflected the afternoon light, creating a rainbow on the roof of the coach.

Tommy grinned, watching fascinated as the colors danced. Relaxing, he let loose of Matthias and climbed up on the seat next to the woman. Quinn, gaining strength from his brother's bravery, leaned forward and held out his hands. Matthias lifted him into the coach.

The woman gave her mirror to Tommy and reached out and set him on the seat beside her.

"You'll take care of my boys," Matthias warned, his voice coated with steel.

Society Miss met his gaze. There was no hint of fear. "I shall take good care of them until you arrive in town."

The faintest hint of her perfume teased his nose. Roses. It had been a long time since he'd smelled the scent of a woman. In the last twelve months since his wife's death, he'd been too busy to miss the sensation of having a woman under him.

Now, he was acutely aware of how long it had been.

Matthias cleared his throat. "Their grandfather

will ride on top. When they get to town, Frank will see that they get to the mercantile and a Mrs. Hilda Clements.''

"Of course," Society Miss said.

For the first time in a good while, Matthias felt as if he was getting a lucky break. Tommy, the little one, nestled next to Society Miss, fascinated by the pearl buttons that trimmed her cuff.

Matthias turned, ready to tackle the wheel of his wagon. He'd taken only a step when he heard the retching sound. He whirled around in time to see Tommy throw up all over Society Miss.

Abby stared down at her now-wet lap as she heard Mr. Stokes shout several oaths. For a moment she thought she'd retch.

Mr. Stokes pressed a cloth to his face. He stood so quickly he bumped his head on top of the wagon. Stepping over her soiled skirt, he pushed past the stranger to get out of the carriage. "Good Lord, I'll bet they have cholera or measles. I'll be riding on the top."

Abby didn't have to look over at the boys' father to know he was still there. His presence filled the silent carriage. The man's fingers tightened on the coach door, and she half expected the brittle wood to crack in his powerful fist.

She looked into the watery, sad eyes of the boy beside her. A mixture of horror and fear straightened his tiny mouth into a grim line as his eyes wavered to his father and then back to her.

Despite Mr. Stokes's declaration, she doubted the boy was ill. She'd heard children often got motion sickness when they rode in wagons. "Let's get this cleaned up."

Managing her best smile, she chucked the boy under the chin and faced the man. To her surprise, the man wasn't angry. Behind his frustration she saw sadness.

Lifting her skirt, she started to climb down.

The man instantly took her elbow.

She stared at his long tapered fingers, calloused by hard labor. His dark eyes cut into her and suddenly the idea of going anywhere with him unsettled.

"It's all right," she reassured the boy. "A damp cloth and it'll be good as new."

The stranger peered past her. "Tommy, you all right, son?"

Tommy shrugged. "I feel good now."

The father shook his head. "That's good. Can you sit tight for a minute with your brother while I clean up this lady?"

"Yes, Pa."

"I'll help her," Frank, the old man, said from behind him. "I know you got that wagon wheel to fix."

"Climb on up to your seat, Frank. I can handle it on my own."

Frank exchanged glances with Holden then reluctantly climbed up top.

He took her hand in his. Through her crocheted black gloves she felt the heat and strength of his fingers. She could feel the color rising in her cheeks.

But the father was all business. Instead of cajoling, he tugged her forward and before she could react banded his long fingers around her narrow waist. Without a word, he lifted her out of the carriage and set her on the hard ground.

Abby stumbled back, shocked at her own reaction. "This really isn't necessary."

Still silent, he pulled a bandanna from his coat pocket and grabbed the hem of her skirt, lifting it so that her petticoats showed.

Abby searched for her voice as she yanked her skirt from his hand. "I am engaged to be married. This kind of interaction can't be proper." She'd not spoken of her engagement out loud before and it sounded strange, so unfamiliar as if she were talking about someone else.

"I don't have time for niceties." He brushed her hand away and finished cleaning the skirt.

The bite in the stranger's tone rankled her nerves. "There's no need to be rude," she said, using the tone she reserved for difficult shopkeepers and surly chimney sweeps.

He looked at her as if she'd grown a third eye. "You want polite, then go back to wherever you came from. I don't have time for it."

"I shall tell my fiancé about this."

He glanced up at Stokes, who still had a handkerchief pressed over his nose. "Your man doesn't look willing to help you."

Abby followed his angry gaze to Mr. Stokes. "Mr. Stokes is *not* my fiancé."

A flicker of surprise flashed in the stranger's eyes but was gone as quickly as it came.

Mr. Stokes shifted in his seat. "Lady, get in the carriage. I want to make town by nightfall."

"Time is wasting, lady," the coachman said.

Irritated, she snatched her skirt back and reached for the handle by the door with the other. Her shoe heel caught on the hem of her skirt and she cursed vanity for choosing to wear her gray Sunday best dress. At the time, she'd wanted to make a good impression on her husband-to-be. But the dress's full skirts and high-heeled shoes, which were fine for church in the city, were completely impractical in Montana. Now she wished she'd remained in her simple calico with the streamlined skirt.

Strong hands again wrapped around her waist. Away from the stifling air of the coach, she caught a whiff of the stranger's masculine scent. No coiling aftershaves or scented soaps like Mr. Stokes. His scent was purely masculine and not unpleasant, she realized.

This stranger had stirred more emotions and reactions in her in the last five minutes than the butcher had in a year. She couldn't say if it were him or that all her senses had been heightened by her unknown future. She hoped her intended didn't make her feel like this, too. She wanted safety and comfort, not passion.

He set her in the carriage and waited until she'd retaken her seat next to the boys. She could still feel his fingers on her as she straightened her skirts.

"Thank you for your help."

"Ma'am." He winked and smiled at the children. The smile vanished when he shifted his gaze to her. He touched the brim of his hat. "I'll see you in town, Miss Smyth. Take good care of my boys."

The softly spoken words were laced with warning. This man protected his own.

A shiver passed down her spin as she wondered

what it felt like to be protected by this man. She swallowed amazed at the direction of her thoughts.

Oily peacocks like Mr. Stokes and hard, dangerous men like this stranger.

What was her new husband going to be like?

Chapter Three

The tingling in Abby's limbs quickly faded when she saw the two boys huddled together on the seat. Both looked pale, their lips drawn into tight lines.

Abby sat next to the boys. She placed her hand on the forehead of the little boy. "What's your name?"

He sniffed, and then popped his thumb in his mouth.

She'd never been around children before. She had no younger brothers or sisters. Joanne, though she was three years younger, was twelve when Abby had moved in.

Of course, she'd seen children of all shapes and sizes in the park with their mothers or nannies, but she'd never actually had to deal with one.

"How does your stomach feel now?" She glanced down at her damp skirt. "Better, I hope."

The little boys stared at her, silent. She waited an extra beat, expecting them to say something. Nothing.

She glanced down at the mirror Tommy held tightly in his dirty hands. "Want to make another rainbow?"

Again, nothing.

Hoping for a better response from the older one she smiled at him. His face was covered in dirt and he looked on the verge of tears. She remembered one of the mothers in a San Francisco park. She'd picked up her son and held him close when he was upset. That child had brightened up instantly.

She reached and picked the little boy up. Before she could lift him on her lap, he started kicking and screaming. She struggled to hold on to him, but he arched his back and started to swing his arms. One pudgy hand caught her in the eye.

Abby put the boy down instantly. The child scrambled back next to his brother and started to cry. She rubbed her injured eye.

Oh Lord, what was she going to do? She'd always assumed she'd be a natural with children. That they'd love her if she were only kind and loving in return.

But these children seemed to hate her.

Nothing Abby said or did would quiet them until

the older one discovered that he could stand on one seat and jump to the other across the aisle. The smaller one's eyes had immediately brightened, and he'd begun to copy his brother. Abby was so relieved that they'd stopped crying that she let them keep jumping. She'd never expected such a mindless pastime would keep boys busy for over an hour.

Finally, they settled on the other seat and lay their heads down. The younger smiled and laid his head against his brother's shoulder. The older patted his brother gently on the leg and they fell asleep. She untied the curtains over the window, dimming the interior of the coach.

A meager ring of light around the edges of the worn fabric provided enough light for Abby to watch the boys. She couldn't help but feel the tug of sadness. The older of the two, who couldn't be four yet, had already learned that he must look after his younger brother. Too young, she thought to be so independent.

Abby had lost her parents at the age of fifteen to cholera. Their loss had slashed through her heart and for a time she'd thought she'd never be able to live without them. But in time, she'd learned to cherish the memories of her parents.

Her mother, Caroline, had been raised in privilege. She'd grown up attending balls and wearing silks. The expectation was that she'd marry into another well-connected family. Instead, she'd done the unpardonable. She'd fallen in love with a young vicar, Richard, who didn't have two wooden nickels to his name, and she'd eloped with him. When her family discovered what she'd done, they'd cut her off completely.

So Abby hadn't grown up with silks or fancy parties. Instead, she'd lived in a simple Arizona parsonage that ministered to miners, harlots and the poor. To her parents' sorrow, her mother had never carried another baby to term. There'd never been much money, but she always had enough to eat and there'd always been plenty of laughter and music. Her father played the fiddle and her mother the piano. Many a night her parents would play while she sang.

Smiling at the memory, she studied the boys. They weren't underfed. Despite the dirt and grime, they looked to be a healthy size. She'd doubted there was music in their house and she couldn't imagine their father laughed often.

Abby let her head drop back against the wall behind her. The now steady rocking of the coach coupled with the silence had her eyes drifting closed. She released a small sigh and let her shoulders sag.

Perhaps she could steal a few minutes of sleep. Just a few minutes.

The coach jerked to a stop.

Her eyes popped open immediately and the boys started awake. Tommy, confused about his surroundings, rolled off the seat and hit the floor with a thud. He started to cry.

Immediately, Abby picked him up. Tired and disoriented, the boy didn't struggle with her this time. Instead he laid his head on her shoulder and popped his thumb into his mouth.

Quinn pushed himself up. His hair stuck straight up and a wrinkle in the cushion had creased the side of his face. He looked around and stuck his lip out.

Abby held her hand out to him and he scrambled off the seat and came to sit beside her. "You two just rest easy. The coach driver should be here to tell us where we are."

Men's voices drifted from above as she heard the driver set the brake. The coach shifted to the right and she heard booted feet hit the ground outside her door before it swung open.

"Welcome to Crickhollow!" Holden the driver said, sweeping his hand wide. His face was deeply tanned by the sun and his eyes were clear and bright.

A fresh batch of butterflies fluttered in Abby's stomach. "Thank you."

"Looks like you and the young ones fared pretty well," said Holden.

Behind him stood the man she'd overheard the boys call Grandpa. "They look right at home in your arms."

Quinn and Tommy both grinned when they saw their grandfather, but neither seemed in a hurry to move away from Abby.

A silent communication passed between Frank and Holden. Both grinned at her as if they were Cheshire cats.

"We did just fine," Abby said sitting a little straighter. She righted her hat, which had slipped too low over her forehead. "I need to find Mrs. Hilda Clements. She is to board me until my fiancé arrives."

Holden unhooked a small block of wood from the side of the carriage and placed it below the door. "Just step right on down, Miss Abigail, and stretch your legs. I know you got to be stiffer than wood after that ride."

Frank leaned in and took the tired boys, while Abby unlocked her joints and rose in the coach, which was only tall enough for her to stand hunched over. Her knees groaned as she moved the few steps to the door. Holden took her hand as she gathered up her skirt and climbed down.

She longed to stretch her arms over her head and work the kinks from her body but realized that would have to wait until she reached Mrs. Clements's house.

Mr. Stokes placed his bowler on his balding head. "Where can I find a place to get a drink?"

Holden nodded toward a small dugout. "That's the saloon. Danny's got good whiskey."

"Excellent." Scratching his chin, he moved slowly toward the saloon.

Abby looked out at the collection of buildings. Just over a half-dozen in all, they sat low to the ground, had pitched roofs and small doorways. Only the one had a window.

The first bubble of alarm rose before reason took over. She glanced from side to side, half expecting to see the rest of the town, where the real buildings were. But to her west there was nothing but the single dusty road that snaked toward the mountains. "This is Crickhollow?"

"Sure is," Holden said, his pride clear. "I know with you coming from the city it may seem a bit small but we're growing by leaps and bounds."

Mr. Barrington's letters had described a thriving town. A growing mercantile, a bustling stagecoach line and populated community. "Growing, did you say?"

"Population fifty-six if you count the homesteaders." He laughed. "Fifty-seven now that you're here."

Despite the cool June air she could feel a trickle of sweat run down her back. She'd walked away from San Francisco right off the end of the earth.

Abby lifted her chin. She even managed a smile. "When will Mr. Barrington arrive?" she said. Her voice sounded surprisingly steady.

Again Holden and Frank exchanged glances.

Frank leaned down and whispered something to the boys, who took off running toward the one building with windows—the mercantile. "He'll be here before the day's out."

"You know my fiancé?" she said.

Frank shifted, clearly uncomfortable. "Everybody knows everybody in the valley."

Just then a portly woman hurried out of the mercantile. She wore black and her graying hair was pulled back in a tight bun. Her white apron flapped in the breeze and she hurried across the dusty street toward them. "I was beginning to worry about you, Holden. You're four hours late."

He shrugged his shoulders. "You name it and it went wrong today."

"The boys okay?" Frank said.

The woman smiled. "I gave them each a piece of candy. They're quite content." The woman looked past him and the boys to Abigail. "Miss Smyth?"

"Yes," Abby said hopefully.

"Welcome! We have been waiting for you." She hurried forward and took Abby by the arm. "You must be exhausted. I've got cookies and tea for you and the boys. Holden, Frank, you want to join us?"

Holden raised up his hand. "I'll pass for the moment. I've got to get the horses changed and get the stage unpacked and repacked. If I'm lucky, I can leave at first light."

Frank's eyes brightened. "Make sure you load my luggage."

Surprised, Abby shifted her gaze to the old man. "You're leaving town?"

"Time I got back east. I only came out here to care for the boys when my daughter became ill. Now that's she's passed there's no need for me to stay."

The boy's didn't have a mother. And their father didn't have a wife. Of course his marital status was none of her business but that didn't stop the ripple of emotion that tingled through her body.

With an effort she forced her mind back to what

really mattered. "Who's going to take care of the boys?" It was none of her business, of course, but Abby wanted to know they'd be cared for.

Mrs. Clements glared at Holden and Frank. "You didn't tell her?"

Holden shoved his hands into his pockets. "I figured it was best the news came from another woman."

"Is something wrong?" Abby said.

Mrs. Clements was the first to recover. "I just thought that these men would have seen to the introductions while you were out on the road."

"There were no introductions," Abby said.

"On the road, the man you met?" Mrs. Clements asked.

"Yes."

Mrs. Clements glanced at the other men, her jaw jutting forward. *Men.* Without fanfare or nonsense, she said, "He is Matthias Barrington. He is your fiancé."

Abby's mind reeled. "He is my fiancé? He didn't say a word to me, and I'm quite sure that I mentioned I was here to meet my intended."

Mrs. Clements's smile was quick and too bright. "Oh, I wouldn't worry about that, dear. He just had a lot on his mind. Everything will be fine as soon as he gets to town."

* * *

It was just past nine the next morning when Matthias pulled his wagon to a stop in front of the Clements's Mercantile. The night chill still clung to the air, and Matthias's back and arms were stiff from sleeping on the ground.

He'd hoped to make town by last night, but the repairs, like most everything else lately, had taken much longer than he'd imagined. By the time he'd finished, the sun was setting on a moonless night. And unless he wanted to risk another broken wheel, his only choice was to bunk down. He knew Mrs. Clements and Frank would look after the boys, so there were no worries there.

Now, as he set the hand brake he realized just how weary he was. He would have traded his soul for a hot bath and eight solid hours of sleep but he had to talk with Frank. Somehow he had to find a way to get his father-in-law to stay another few months.

As he hopped down, he was struck that things weren't as they should be. The wind blew as it always did, but Mr. Clements and Danny weren't sitting out front of the saloon, as they were most mornings. And there was no sign of Holden's coach.

Matthias's gut clenched. Something was wrong. The boys.

He strode straight to Mrs. Clements's store. A blast of warm air and the smell of bacon and biscuits greeted him as he stepped into the store. Children's laughter drifted out from behind the army blanket that separated the shop from Mrs. Clements's living space. The tightness around his heart eased. The boys were fine and for the first time in a good while, they sounded happy.

Suddenly, the memory of his late wife sliced through the fatigue and worry. Elise's laugh had been clear and bright, like church bells. No matter how many worries he had, his mood had always lightened when she laughed.

Matthias shoved aside the thoughts that only made his days feel longer.

He pulled off his hat and started down the center aisle cut between rows of barrels filled with flour, sugar and dried beans. In front of him, a plywood counter was piled high with cans of peaches, a jug of white lightning, tin cups and a scale for measuring sugar and spices. From low-lying rafters hung buckets, baskets and three lanterns.

"Mrs. Clements?" Matthias called out.

The storekeeper emerged from the curtained door behind the counter, her blue calico dress and a white apron hugging her full hips. Her hair was piled high on her head in a loose topknot. "Ah, you finally made it. Frank was a little worried when you didn't arrive by nightfall. I told him not to worry. Chores always take twice as long as we ever imagine plus you're as tough as a mountain goat.''

"Where is everyone?"

"Mr. Clements was called out of town three days ago—delivery to Ephraim Collier's ranch. And Mr. Stokes went with him so he could have a look at Collier's stock.''

"Who is Stokes?"

"That greenhorn on the stage. Turns out he's with the railroad, looking for ranchers to supply him with beef and horses.''

Matthias flexed his fingers, tight with tension. "Of all times to break a wagon wheel.''

Mrs. Clements's eyes brightened as if she could read his mind. "Don't worry, he'll be back in early July. I told him your horse flesh was the finest in the valley.''

If he were going to show the man his stock, he'd have to spend the next month rounding them up. More work. And still not enough time.

"Thank you." He ran his fingers through his hair. "Where's Frank?"

Her eyes dimmed a fraction. "Why, Frank left with Holden at first light on the stage. He's on his way to Salt Lake.''

Shock and bitter disappointment tightened his throat. "I'd wanted to speak to him before he left."

The anger in his voice had her smile fading a fraction. "He said you two had talked a good bit already."

His fingers bit into the rim of his hat. They'd talked but to his way of thinking, they'd not come to a satisfactory conclusion. "Damnation."

"I'm sorry," she said quietly.

Matthias shoved out a sigh, tamping down the anger coiling in his gut. Frank was gone and there was no sense worrying about what couldn't be fixed. Time to cut his losses. "I've a list of supplies," he said, his tone as matter-of-fact as he could manage.

"Of course. Holden brought in some fresh supplies. A few candies and couple of bolts of a nice thick wool."

Matthias hoped by the end of the summer when he took his cattle and horses to the railhead there'd be money for a few extras but for now every cent counted. "Just the basics this trip."

Again, children's laughter drifted out from behind the curtain. He was surprised the boys hadn't come running when he'd first spoken. Then he heard a woman's soft voice speaking to them. This last year the boys gravitated toward women—a sure sign they missed their mother.

For just a moment, he imagined Elise holding the boys, singing to them as she did when they were real little.

But when the curtain opened, it wasn't Elise but Society Miss who was staring at him.

Disappointment slashed at his heart.

He'd forgotten all about Society Miss.

He nodded his head. "Ma'am."

She'd gotten rid of that awful hat and changed out of that fancy traveling dress into a simple calico. Her cheeks looked pinker, a sign that she'd picked up some sun yesterday. She'd also unpinned her hair and tied it back at the nape of her neck with a simple ribbon. Her hair was thick, lush and despite a slight curl nearly reached her narrow waist. He imagined it felt like silk.

The smell of roses drifted around him again. His gut tightened and he grew hard. His body was letting him know loud and clear that it had been a long time since he'd been with a woman.

"I'd like you to meet Miss Abigail Smyth from San Francisco," Mrs. Clements said.

Miss Smyth nodded as a faint blush colored her cheeks. "It's a pleasure to meet you formally, Mr. Barrington."

"Ma'am."

Miss Smyth smiled. "Things were rather hectic by the wagon yesterday. No time for formal introductions."

"No, I suppose not." As much as he liked her feminine scent, he was burning daylight. There was a lot of work to do before the sunset today. "Pleasure meeting you. Thank you for your help with the boys."

"They're good children."

"Yes."

She looked as if she wanted to say something else. Another time he would have indulged in the conversation. He liked the sound of her voice. But he turned away from her now. He had more important matters on his mind.

"Mrs. Clements, can I talk to you outside?"

Mrs. Clements glanced at Society Miss. "Here's fine, Matthias."

He didn't like airing his business in front of strangers. "I need to talk to you about the boys."

Mrs. Clements didn't look interested in stepping outside. "Go ahead."

"With Frank gone and all, I'm in a bind. I was hoping they could board with you for the summer."

He heard Miss Smyth's sharp intake of breath.

No doubt, Miss Smyth thought him hardhearted for sending his children away. He couldn't blame her.

Mrs. Clements's smile faded to embarrassment. "Before we talk about that, there is another more pressing matter you and I need to discuss."

"Is there a problem with those renegades again?" he said. So much anger and frustration bunched his muscles now he wouldn't have minded a fight to work off the heat inside him.

"Oh, no, nothing like that. There's a matter you and I need to discuss."

Discuss. Hilda Clements could talk a man's ears off if given half the chance. He decided to head her off. But before he could answer, Miss Smyth spoke.

"I thought caring for the boys was going to be my job."

He swung his gaze to meet hers. He was certain that he'd heard wrong. "Ma'am?"

She held his gaze, though he sensed she was nervous. Still she pulled back her shoulders. "I mean, since I am going to be your wife, it only seems right that the children stay with us."

For a moment, his head swam as if a prizefighter had landed a knockout punch. "My what?"

Mrs. Clements stepped forward, wearing a broad grin that hinted at trouble. "Miss Smyth *is* the bit of news I was referring to."

Matthias's head started to throb. The last thing he needed was a riddle. "What the devil are you talking about, Mrs. Clements?"

The older woman smoothed her hands over her white apron and cleared her throat. "We ordered you a wife. Miss Smyth is your fiancée."

Chapter Four

"*You ordered a what?*" Matthias shouted.

Abby started at the sound of Mr. Barrington's bellow. His voice, rich and full of anger, hinted at a man who was used to giving orders, a man who didn't like surprises.

She watched the color drain from Mr. Barrington's face and his full lips flatten in a thin grim line.

He hadn't been expecting her.

Of course, it all made sense now. On the road yesterday and moments ago when he'd arrived he'd acted as though she was a complete stranger to him. Which of course, she was. Why hadn't Mrs. Clements told her the truth last night?

For a moment her knees nearly buckled. She'd come so far, and given up so much. For what? A lie. "Mrs. Clements, what do you mean, *we* ordered you a wife? Who is *we?*"

Mr. Barrington glared down at the older woman. The children's voices drifted from behind the curtain. He lowered his voice. "Very good question."

There was no hint of remorse in Mrs. Clements's eyes. "Frank, Holden and I decided you needed a wife," she said, her tone clipped and practical.

"Tell me this is a joke," Mr. Barrington said, his voice laced with fury.

Abby closed her eyes, clinging to her composure. If this was a joke, she was the one who'd been fooled.

Mrs. Clements's smile remained intact but her gaze reflected steel. "No mistake, Matthias. We put an ad in the *San Francisco Morning Chronicle.*"

"Was *she* in on this?" he asked, jabbing his thumb toward Abby.

Annoyance flickered in Abby. Her life was dissolving into a mess and Mr. Barrington was blaming her. "I can assure you, I had no idea. I believed your letter...*the* letters to be genuine and from you." Abby pressed her hand to her unsettled stomach. Now she understood why Mrs. Clements had artfully dodged many of her questions last night.

Mr. Barrington's gaze pinned her. "What letters?"

The heat in his blue eyes made Abby take a step back before she turned and went to her reticule. Frustrated by her cowardice, she pulled out a neat bundle of four letters tied together with a blue ribbon. Anger and frustration quickened her step. "Letters from you."

He took the letters and thumbed through them, before he handed them back to her. His warm fingers brushed hers. There was nothing tender about his touch. Strictly matter-of-fact. "They are not from me."

Abby lifted an eyebrow. It took everything in her not to run screaming from the room. "Yes, I surmised that much."

Her sarcasm seemed to catch him by surprise. She imagined a glimmer of respect in his eyes.

"I wrote the letters," Mrs. Clements said. "I acted on your behalf, Matthias."

Mr. Barrington's face looked as if it had been etched from granite. "Why would you stick your nose into my life? I did not ask you to do anything like that." His voice rose again.

Mrs. Clements shrugged, but she did take a half step back. "You've done so much for everyone in the valley and you've been struggling so since Elise died. You are not the kind of man who asks for favors, so we took matters into our own hands."

"Did anyone stop to think that I don't *want* a wife?" he said tersely.

"In Montana one must be practical. It's not always about what we want," the older woman shot back.

Abby felt as insignificant and unwanted as she had in her uncle's house. "Mr. Barrington, perhaps we need a moment to talk alone."

Mr. Barrington speared her with a hard look. "Look, Miss…"

"Smyth," she supplied.

He rubbed the back of his neck, clearly tired and very frustrated. "We have nothing to discuss."

Abby blinked at Mr. Barrington. "I beg to differ. There is a great deal to discuss, considering I just uprooted my life to be here."

He was clearly a man who relished control. He worked his jaw and tipped his head back to stare at the ceiling as if he were trying to keep his temper in check. "When will Holden be back, Mrs. Clements?" He fired the question like a bullet.

Mrs. Clements tucked her hands in the deep pockets of her apron. "He said he'd be gone at least a week."

"If he's smart he'll stay away a hell of a lot longer. It'll take longer than a week for my anger to cool on this one,'' he said. ''Damn his scrawny hide.''

Abby pinched the bridge of her nose. At this moment, she was sorely tempted to take the last three dollars she had and buy a stage ticket to anywhere. The unknown was far more appealing than Mr. Barrington at the moment. But like it or not, she was stuck. ''Mr. Barrington, you and I really do need to discuss this matter.''

He swung his gaze to her. ''Lady, you were brought here under false pretenses and for that I'm truly sorry. But I'm not marrying you.''

Pride had her lifting her chin a notch. ''Nor was I expecting you to.''

''Good.'' He stared at her with bone-jarring intensity. Never had a man looked at her so intently. A soft shiver danced down her spine.

''Matthias…Abby,'' Mrs. Clements said sweetly. ''I think you're both being a bit hasty. Miss Abby is right. You need time alone to get to know each other.''

He rubbed the back of his neck with his hand. ''Time is the one thing I don't have, Mrs. Clements. I got two boys to raise and a ranch to run. I don't have time to be a nursemaid, let alone court a city woman.''

Abby clenched her fists. "I am not helpless, Mr. Barrington."

He let his gaze roam the length of her body. "Lady, you don't know the first thing about life out here."

"I've learned many skills in my life. Montana is no different than many of the other challenges I've faced."

He lifted a gaze. "That so?"

"Absolutely," she said all bravado as she stepped toward him. Inches away, the energy from his body radiated.

"So you know all there is to know about working back-breaking hours, milking cows, planting gardens, churning butter and chopping wood."

In truth, she didn't know a lot about those things. "I know about hard work."

"That doesn't cut it. And I don't have the time to teach you." He swung his dark gaze to Mrs. Clements, dismissing Abby completely. "Put Miss Smyth up and when Holden arrives she can catch the next stage home. I've got a ranch to tend."

Abby grabbed his arm. The muscles tightened like steel. "You can't dismiss me like this. I've come too far to turn back now." He was her only real connection to this land—the man she'd thought she'd marry. And Uncle Stewart would never take her back a second time, nor would she ask him.

For a moment she imagined his eyes softened before a wall of ice descended over them. "I'd help you if I could, lady. But I can't."

The boys' voices had grown silent. She imagined they were on the other side of the curtain listening to every word. She wondered how much of this they understood.

Mrs. Clements started to stack the can of peaches in a neat triangle. "Like it or not, Matthias," she said, "you need a wife."

"I *had* a wife," he bit back.

"You loved Elise, but she's dead and gone," the older woman said softly. She jabbed her thumb toward the curtain behind her. Their laughter had stopped. "But those boys of yours need a mother. And you need a helpmate."

"We're surviving."

"Not for long. You're running out of choices," Mrs. Clements said.

Sadness rose in Abby. This scene was nothing like what she'd pictured. If she had a lick of sense, she'd follow her first inclination.

But she didn't.

Abby was through hiding in the kitchens and watching life pass her by. "Excuse me for saying this, Mr. Barrington, but you and the boys don't look like you're doing so well.''

Anger flashed in his eyes. "How the hell would you know?'' he roared.

Quinn and Tommy appeared at the curtain then. Their freshly scrubbed faces tight with worry, their gazes darted between their father and Abby. They were holding the rag balls she'd made for them last night. She'd never imagined a handful of rags could be so entertaining.

"Pa?'' Quinn said. He ran to his father with his younger brother on his heels.

"It's all right, son,'' Mr. Barrington said. He stabbed his fingers through his hair. It was clear he hated seeing the worry in their young eyes. "What's that you've got in your hand?''

"Ball,'' Tommy said.

Quinn held his up proudly. "Miss Abby made it.''

He brushed a lock of clean hair off Tommy's face. "Who cleaned you up?''

"Miss Abby.''

Mr. Barrington's gaze locked on her for an instant. Dark blue eyes reflected a mixture of gratitude, anger and frustration.

Abby looked past Mr. Barrington to Mrs. Clements. "Would you do us a small favor and take the boys outside? The boys can toss their new balls, while Mr. Barrington and I talk.''

Mrs. Clements hustled around the side of her counter. ''That's an excellent idea. You two just need time alone.'' She took Tommy from Mr. Barrington and grasped Quinn's little hand. ''Come on boys, let's play a game of toss with those fancy new toys of yours.''

Tommy started to whimper and reached out to his father. ''No.''

Mrs. Clements kept moving toward the door. ''I've a new horse you two boys haven't seen yet.''

Tommy stopped whimpering immediately. ''Horse.''

''That's right,'' she said as she opened the door. ''I bought him off an Indian. He's got white and brown spots.''

The door closed behind them. Abby could still hear Mrs. Clements's cheery voice but it quickly faded until nothing remained but an uncomfortable silence.

Abby shifted her gaze from the door to Mr. Barrington. Dark circles smudged under his eyes and three or four days' growth of beard covered his square jaw.

''I thank you for what you've done for my boys, but I don't want a wife.''

She was used to not being wanted. But she understood her value. "But you *need* one."

He shoved out a deep breath. "I'll make it without one."

"Pride is a wonderful thing, Mr. Barrington, but there is a time and place for it. Believe me, mine has taken a sore beating today. This is not how I pictured our first meeting."

Frowning, he shoved his fingers through his hair. "I'm sorry for that, Miss Smyth. If I'd known what Mrs. Clements and the others were up to, I'd have stopped it instantly. But that doesn't change anything."

She shrugged, trying to look casual when she felt anything but as she watched her dreams fall apart. "I have spent the last ten years swallowing my pride and doing what was practical. I'd leave now if I had any other options. I severed all my ties with my family to move out here. Going back is not a choice for me, even if I did have the money to finance the trip."

He shook his head. "Miss Smyth, I am sorry—" He stopped himself. "You are better off trying your luck in the marriage mart somewhere else."

She swallowed, her throat tight. She wouldn't leave now. "I disagree. We can help each other. I am a hard worker, and I already have affection for the boys."

Suddenly he looked very weary. "You are not their mother."

His words were true but they stung nonetheless. "That does not change the fact that they need a woman to care for them. Mrs. Clements has already told you she can't watch the boys."

Anger flashed in his blue eyes. And then just as suddenly it was gone. He rubbed the back of his neck with his hand. "Miss Smyth, I don't doubt that you are sincere and that you mean well. But this land chews young women up and spits them out. Montana will wring the life out of you and make you sorry you ever came to this place."

Had his first wife felt this way? "I've survived a lot, Mr. Barrington. Don't underestimate me."

"Frank is a strong man, but after one Montana winter he was desperate to leave."

"He is old. And this place claimed his daughter." She moved closer slowly until she was less than a foot from him. "This is a land that's full of possibilities for me."

"Elise, my wife, said the same thing before we moved out here. Within a year, she'd grown to hate the place."

"She said that?"

"She never would admit it, but I knew."

He may have loved his first wife, but she suspected it had not been a successful partnership. "I am not your late wife."

"No."

"When I was nine, my parents opened a mission in the Arizona territory. We lived in a small adobe with dirt floors the first year. A half-mile walk separated our house from fresh water. Every morning, we had to shake out our shoes in case scorpions had nested in our shoes overnight. We stayed for six years and those were some of the happiest times of my life."

He stared down at her as if he were really looking at her for the first time. "I swore on my wife's grave I'd never subject another wife to Montana— that I'd never marry again."

She felt as if a door had cracked open in his heart. She sensed he was a man who rarely shared his feelings yet he was telling her. "I'm up to the challenge."

Abruptly, he stood and walked to the window. He was silent for long, tense seconds. "Thank you for washing the boys."

His gratitude caught her off guard. She walked closer to the window. Outside, directly in front of the store, the boys were taking turns tossing their balls to Mrs. Clements. "Quinn couldn't sleep because his skin itched so I decided to clean them both up. The bathwater was black by the time I finished with them."

"Thank you. I've not been able to nurture them much lately."

"You can't do it all, Mr. Barrington." To her relief, her voice sounded steady and didn't reflect her fear.

He sighed, and she sensed he'd come to a decision. He faced her. For a long time he was silent and she thought he might not have heard her. "I'm willing to hire you on for the summer. I can't pay until the roundup in the fall, but I'm good for it. With the money, you can leave the valley, find a new home."

Abby straightened her shoulders. "I came here to be your wife, not your servant."

His body stiffened. "It's the best I can offer."

She'd compromised so much in her aunt and uncle's house. She'd never complained about her attic room or when her aunt had asked her to start working in the kitchen. She'd stayed silent when her cousin had had so many coming-out parties. "I came here for marriage."

She imagined she saw challenge in his eyes. "It's the one thing I won't give."

"I'd be a good wife to you."

He shook his head. "I'm not the kind of husband any woman would want."

He was wrong. Judging by what she'd seen so far, he was an honest man, proud and strong. "Why would you say that?"

He started to pace. "I've got a ranch that has promise but if I don't bring in the herd and sell it for a decent profit this fall, I lose everything. I've got two half-wild boys and more work than I could handle."

"Exactly why you need me."

"*Exactly* why you should be running from me." A pain still fresh burned in his eyes. "I could never love you. My heart died with Elise."

"Perhaps in time, there could be some affection."

"Not from me." His broad shoulders tightened a fraction. "You deserve better than me, Miss Smyth."

She eyed him. A thick lock of hair had fallen over his forehead, making him look a little softer, younger. She wondered what he'd been like before his wife died. Had he laughed? "At least you are honest."

A half smile tipped the edge of his mouth. "It's about all I've got left."

"I value honesty. I've dealt with my share of liars who were quite willing to tell me what I wanted to hear to get what they wanted. You haven't done that."

"What are you getting at?"

He needed time. "I'll live at your ranch for the summer. I'll care for the boys, but I won't come as a hired hand. I'll be coming to see if marriage between us is possible."

"It isn't."

"Time will tell."

He lifted an eyebrow. "You'd live with a man without marriage?"

"My reputation is the least of my concerns now. And from what I've heard from Mrs. Clements, out here a woman does what she must."

"I mean what I say, Miss Smyth. I don't want another marriage."

"I'm betting time will change that."

"At the end of the summer if I haven't changed my mind, you'll leave."

Her stomach clenched. The idea of leaving bothered her more than she imagined. "Yes."

He stared at her as if trying to read her mind. "I sure could use the help on the ranch." He hesitated, as if scrambling for any reason not to take her on.

Finally, he reluctantly held out his hand to her. "Okay, I accept your terms."

She took it. Strong, calloused fingers wrapped around her hand. Warmth fizzled through her, but she was careful to keep her feelings hidden. Suddenly, she wondered what it would feel like to kiss Mr. Barrington. He had full lips. Handsome lips.

As if he'd read her mind, he released her hand and stepped back. "All right. I'll take you on for the summer. Beyond that, I'm not making any promises."

Warmth colored her cheeks. "Understood."

"I don't want the boys knowing why you are here. As far as they are concerned, you are here for the summer. I don't want them getting their hopes up over something that won't be happening."

Unexpected tears tightened her throat. "I understand."

"Let's get your things packed and head on back to the ranch." He turned and left.

Abby chided her schoolgirl desire.

This was a business arrangement for Mr. Barrington, even if she wanted more.

The reality of her life smacked head-on into the dreams she'd nurtured for so long. It would be so easy to feel sorry for herself. But she refused. She'd do what she'd always done.

Somehow, she'd make it work.

Chapter Five

"Daddy, why is the lady here?" Quinn said.

Abby stiffened as she stared down at the boy who sat next to his brother. Both children were wedged between her and Mr. Barrington on the front seat of the buckboard. She'd promised Mr. Barrington she'd not tell the boys all the details of their arrangement and she would honor her pledge. She waited for him to answer.

Mr. Barrington tightened his hands on the reins. He didn't answer immediately, as if he were hoping the question would simply be forgotten.

Quinn laid his small hand on his father's arm. "Daddy, why is the lady here?"

Mr. Barrington shifted in his seat, clearly uncomfortable.

Abby managed a smile. "I'll be helping your pa some."

Mr. Barrington relaxed his hold on the reins a fraction as if relieved.

Tommy popped his thumb in his mouth and stared at her. "But why?"

"He's got a lot of work to do," she said.

"Where's Grandpa?" Quinn said.

"Grandpa's gone back to his family in the east," Mr. Barrington said. "In a faraway place called Missouri." Anger still smoldered in his voice when he spoke about Frank.

"Is he coming back?" the older boy said.

Mr. Barrington sighed. "I don't think so."

Abby stared out at the clusters of budding trees that lined the road. Water from a creek splashed nearby. The beauty of the land seemed to breathe life into her, and if this situation weren't so tense she'd have savored it all.

Quinn nervously picked at a loose thread on his pants. The boys seemed to sense the tension between their father and her. "The lady gave us a bath. She made us wash behind our ears."

A hint of a smile tugged the edge of Mr. Barrington's lips. "Good, you needed one."

"I don't like baths," Quinn said. "I like dirt."

"Me too," Tommy said.

"Don't believe them," Abby said, grateful to have something to talk about. She couldn't help but smile when she remembered the two of them in the copper tub. They'd splashed in the water and made bubbles with the soap. "They loved it."

"Well, the tub is like the ocean," Quinn said.

Mr. Barrington lifted an eyebrow.

"I told them about the ocean when they were in the tub. About the waves crashing on the rocky shore, about lighthouses, and the tall ships that sailed into the harbor."

"Lighthouses blink all night long," Quinn said, proud that he remembered.

"Why's that?" Abby said.

"To save the ships," Quinn said, sitting taller.

"Ships!" Tommy shouted.

Mr. Barrington nodded. "I've heard the ocean is a sight to behold."

"You've never been to the ocean?"

"No."

The small fact reminded her just how little she knew about Mr. Barrington. Mrs. Clements had written about many things when she'd forged Mr. Barrington's courtship letters. There'd been descriptions of the valley and the mountains. She'd talked about the rail coming in soon and of the growing town, but it struck Abby now that there'd been few facts about Mr. Barrington, the man.

She wanted to know more about him. Where had he lived as a child? What brought him to Montana?

But as much as she wanted to ask the questions, she understood that until they knew each other a little better, she'd best keep them to herself.

"I moved to the coast when I was fifteen," she said. "Quite a change from the Arizona desert." Perhaps if she talked about herself, he'd offer bits of information about himself. "The wind carries the sound of the ships' horns, the smells of sea and salt and a warm breeze. It's a lovely place. I would sit for hours watching the ships sail in and out of the harbor, wondering what stories the sailors had to tell."

Mr. Barrington nodded, but he kept his eyes ahead. Silence settled between them, as thick and powerful as the mountains in the distance.

Abby broke through it. "Of course, I only got to the wharf on shopping days. I spent most of my days working in a kitchen. Breads are my specialty. I've won prizes for my jams. But I must confess that my laundry and sewing skills are passable at best."

Nothing.

"Still, I am a quick learner." Silence. This was going to be a long ride. She pushed Quinn's hand away from the loose thread. At the rate he was going he'd unravel half the pant leg.

Tommy and Quinn yawned. Soon they'd be asleep. Both, still tired from their trip into town, needed their sleep. But she hated the idea of moving them to the back of the wagon. They'd been a buffer between Mr. Barrington and her.

It struck her then that there'd been no discussion about their sleeping arrangements. Of course, he didn't expect her to share a bed with him, did he? After her debacle with Douglas, she'd promised there'd be nothing like *that* again until she was safely wed. Douglas's touch had always been pleasant, never memorable and never worth the trouble she'd endured as the result. Yet, the idea of doing those same things with Mr. Barrington had heat rising in her cheeks.

She imagined that when Mr. Barrington kissed a woman, she felt it all the way down to the tips of her toes. His hands weren't soft like Douglas's but calloused and rough. When he whispered in a woman's ear, he didn't parrot pretty lies, but spoke of the dark and erotic, much as the servants did when they giggled about their adventures in the bedroom.

Her nerves danced with tension. She jerked her

thoughts back to the present. Lord, what was she doing?

Despite Mr. Barrington's lack of interest in conversation, Abby decided conversation remained the safest course for now. "Mrs. Clements said the railroad might be building tracks through here soon. She said the rail will bring in more miners and farmers and that it'll only help Holden's stagecoach business."

"I suppose that's right."

She tapped her fingers on her knee. "How will it help you?"

"I've got horses and beef to sell."

"How far is your ranch from town?"

"Close."

Like pulling teeth. "How close is close?"

"Five or six hours."

In the city, close was measured in blocks, not hours. Inwardly she groaned. After her long journey from San Francisco, she'd be happy when her travels were at an end. "What does the ranch look like?"

"Like most others."

Frustrated by his lack of interest, she blurted, "Squeezing blood from a turnip would be easier than getting information out of you, Mr. Barrington."

He glanced at her, his eyes sharp with annoyance. "Not much for chitchat, I suppose."

"So I am discovering."

"If you want to talk then go back to San Francisco, Miss Smyth."

"I don't wish to rehash what we've already discussed, Mr. Barrington." She sat a little straighter. "I'm not leaving Montana. I'm here to stay."

Here to stay.

Guilt ate into Matthias. He'd made the only practical decision that he could, but he felt as if were letting Elise down by bringing another woman into the home that he'd built for her.

This asinine plan of Mrs. Clements's had created trouble he didn't need.

As they drove closer to his ranch, the idea of having Abby Smyth under his roof was becoming all too real. His place had once seemed a practical size but with each turn of the wagon wheel it seemed to shrink. There'd be no ignoring her when she moved into the cabin.

The fact was he was drawn to Miss Smyth.

He glanced sideways at her. There was never a woman more opposite from his Elise. Elise had been small-boned, while this Abigail was tall and broad-shouldered. Her eyes weren't smoky or coy but direct and strong.

Elise had always looked her finest when she was in her Sunday best, whereas the simpler clothes suited Miss Smyth. She'd moved stiffly in the yards of fabric yesterday as if the role of a lady had not suited her. But in the calico, she walked with confidence.

Elise had been so young and fresh-faced when they'd moved out here. Her laugh had been quick and when she'd sang it was about the prettiest thing he'd ever heard. She couldn't cook worth a lick and she burned his share of shirts, but in those days he hadn't cared.

When he'd gotten the itch to move west, Elise hadn't wanted to move away from St. Louis. She liked her friends, her social functions and the convenience of a big city. But a homestead in Montana had been a dream of his for years and so he'd worked hard to sell her on the idea. In the end he'd convinced her to go with him.

No one had convinced Miss Smyth to move here. She'd come on her own, which proved either she possessed strength and grit or that she was a fool.

Still, it hadn't been her strength he'd noticed yesterday when he'd wrapped his hands around her narrow waist and lifted her from the carriage. The full curve of her breasts, her scent, the way his body had hardened when she'd been close—those were the things he'd noticed.

Last night when he'd been lying in the back of the wagon staring at the stars, he'd thought about Miss Smyth. He'd imagined desire in her eyes as he skimmed his hand under her skirt, up the inside of her soft leg. He'd imagined she'd been wet and waiting for him. He'd dreamed of unfastening the buttons between her breasts and pushing the fabric aside to kiss her nipples until they'd hardened. He'd dreamed of driving into her until she'd moaned with desire.

Matthias jerked his attention back to the present. Good Lord, he'd all but forgotten Elise for those few moments. He shifted in his seat, annoyed that he was stiff as a poker.

With Miss Smyth as his only source of help for the foreseeable future, the last thing he needed was to have lust singing in his veins.

Hiring her was the right thing to do. It made good sense. He needed help on the ranch and the boys needed someone to look after them.

But knowing all that didn't erase the guilt that had burrowed into his bones.

They arrived at the ranch minutes before sunset. Several hours earlier, Abby and the boys had moved from the front of the wagon to a small pallet in the back. Though it had been a relief to move away from the stone-faced Mr. Barrington, her limbs were now stiffer than ever.

Wincing, she rose slowly so as not to wake the boys. Mr. Barrington had already hopped down from the wagon and was unlatching the back gate.

She climbed over the front seat and down the side of the wagon. Her legs felt wobbly as she stamped her feet and tried to get the blood flowing back in them. She grabbed her belongings, still bundled in her grandmother's tablecloth.

As she scanned the moonlit yard, her gaze settled on her new home. She remembered Mrs. Clements's description of the Barrington homestead. *A fine home, large by Montana standards, with room for a growing family.* But as she stared at the house made of roughly hewn logs, her first impression was that it was a shed built to hold tools. "Mr. Barrington, where's the house?"

"This is it," he said, his voice gruff.

Stunned, her gaze skimmed back to the small stoop, a tin washbasin hanging by the front door and the shingled roof. Five white chickens scratched in the dirt by a large woodpile and a large stump with an ax driven into its center. In the distance a dog barked. The air had grown cold enough to see her breath.

"Go ahead and have a look inside," Mr. Barrington said. "There's a lantern by the front door."

Hugging her belongings wrapped in her tablecloth, Abby moved to the front porch where she found the lantern and matches. She lit the wick, hoping that with a little extra light the place would acquire charm.

It didn't.

Faded blue curtains dangled in the two dirt-streaked windows. Flower boxes hung under each window, but each was filled with weeds. The railing beside the front three stairs was sturdy but the front steps creaked as she climbed up to the front door.

She pushed open the front door and glanced briefly down at the threshold. In her dreams, her husband had whisked her up in his arms and carried her over it.

Faced with the reality of her life, she pushed aside the sad, lonely feeling and stepped over it into her new home.

Immediately, she was struck by the strong ashy scent from the cookstove and the stale scent of male. Holding the lantern high, she inspected the cabin.

If the outside were troubling, the inside was truly frightening.

The rectangular room was perhaps thirty feet wide. At one end there was a large bed with rumpled sheets. By their graying color, Abby would have bet they'd not been washed since last summer. At the other end were a cookstove, a small all-purpose table and four chairs.

The stove had gone cold. On the cooktop sat cast-iron pots, one crusted with what looked like the remains of a stew and the other fried eggs. A slab of ham hung from the low-lying ceiling from a hook. To the right there was a washbasin filled with more dirty plates and cups and above it a narrow shelf with a crock filled with salt.

Queasy at the thought of cleaning this mess, Abby set her bundle down on the table and turned toward the other end of the cabin. There was a ladder that led to a loft. She climbed the ladder and inspected the space. It was outfitted with a small pallet.

Every bone in her body ached with weeks of nervous anticipation and travel. She thought longingly about her bed back at her aunt and uncle's house. The small attic room seemed like a palace now, her small warm bed a haven.

Climbing down, she tried to imagine herself living out the rest of her years in such a place with two growing boys and a man who didn't want her.

The sound of tiny claws scurrying across the bare wood floor echoed in the cabin. A black rodent disappeared through a hole in the floorboard.

A rat! She screamed and jumped back. Immediately, she began to search around her for any other little beasties that might be lurking.

"Ready to leave yet?" Mr. Barrington's deep voice sounded directly behind her.

Startled by the sound of his voice, she turned. The man moved as quiet as a cat. "There is a rat in your cabin."

He held the two sleeping boys in his arms. "A couple, more likely. I've not had time to set traps."

Abby stared at him as if he'd lost his mind.

Moving past her, he strode across the room toward the bed. Gently, he lay both children down.

Quinn stirred for a moment. "Pa?"

Mr. Barrington smoothed back the hair off the boy's face, then tucked the blanket under his chin. "Go on to sleep now, boy, we're home."

"Good," Quinn said.

Mr. Barrington started at each boy a beat longer and then rose. In the dimming light his face was all angles and shadows. "You didn't answer my question."

She couldn't read his expression but there was no missing the challenge in his voice. "What question?"

He took a step forward. "Are you ready to leave?"

Smoothing her damp palms down her skirt she concentrated on keeping her voice steady. "Why should I? The place is lovely."

He let the seconds tick by, then shook his head. "You're a bad liar. But I suppose that's a good thing."

It was a backhanded compliment at best, still it pleased her.

"We both best get to bed," he said. "Tomorrow, like every other day out here, is going to be a long one."

The mention of bed swept away her fatigue and had her nerves dancing. "Where do we sleep?" Grateful for the fading light, she could feel the color burning her face.

"I'll bunk with the boys for now. You can have Frank's loft," he said quickly. "It'll give you some privacy."

She glanced up toward the loft. She prayed she didn't roll out of it in her sleep. "Okay."

"Do you have any other bags?"

She retrieved her bundle. "No, this is all I have."

"It's light for such a long trip."

She shrugged, unwilling to discuss her midnight flight from her uncle's house. "I don't need much."

His eyes narrowed. "You running from the law?"

A grim smile twisted her lips. "No. But there's no going back for me."

The news deepened his scowl. "Don't expect any happy endings out here, Abby. What's between us is strictly business." He turned and left through the front door.

Large tears welled in her eyes. Tipping her head back she refused to let them fall. Her lantern in hand, she climbed the small ladder to the loft. On her knees, she stared at her new room. The loft's crude floor was covered with a pallet and several thick quilts. There was just enough room for one person to sleep.

She thought about her nightgown, her brush and tooth powder still wrapped in her tablecloth. She longed to wash the grime of the day off and brush out her hair, but in the darkness the task was impossible.

This day was over as far as she was concerned and she was glad of it.

Her clothes and shoes still on, she crawled up on the pallet and, lying down, she pulled the blankets up to her chin. Using her bundle as a pillow she put her head down. She blew out her lantern.

Despite her exhaustion, thoughts collided in her mind. Outside she heard an animal howl. Tales of wolves mauling pioneers dug their way out of her memory.

"Look at it this way, Abby," she whispered. "It can't get worse."

The next morning, it got worse.

Chapter Six

When Abby woke hours before dawn, she was freezing. The roof overhead creaked and groaned and a cold chill whisked through the loft. She burrowed deeper under the thick quilts.

For the last ten years, she'd risen before dawn to begin breakfast. In San Francisco the mornings had been her favorite time. A little peace and quiet, just her, her pots and pastry recipes before the day began.

But here the day's tasks felt as formidable as the mountains she'd crossed.

Abby had told Mr. Barrington Montana would not get the better of her. But she'd never prove that to him lying in bed.

Abby rose from the bed and reached for the lantern and match. She lit the wick. Squinting against the light, she wished she could sleep another half hour, even as she tossed back the covers. Because of the rat, she'd kept her clothes and her boots on all last night. Rubbing her hands on her arms, she summoned the courage and climbed down the ladder to survey her kitchen.

Mr. Barrington's deep, even breathing filled the quiet cabin and like a moth to a flame she turned and looked toward his bed. He lay on his side, his long muscular body filling the bed. His arm was draped over the boys, who huddled close for warmth. There was no doubt the man loved his sons.

Smiling, Abby turned from the scene. Her smile vanished when she saw the supplies from town, unloaded by Mr. Barrington last night, littering the floor. Sacks of flour, beans and sugar were piled high on boxes that contained tins filled with fruits and vegetables. She'd need more light to sort through the goods, so she maneuvered past the store-bought goods to the kitchen.

Abby set her lantern down on the shelf above the cold stove. As she turned to search for kindling and matches she stumbled over a child's shoe. She lurched forward and caught herself on the kitchen table. A plate on the table rattled like a church bell.

A few choice words she'd learned from the cook staff came to mind.

In the silence, her toe throbbing she heard Mr. Barrington turn over in his bed. She peered past the glow of lantern light into the darkness and watched him roll to his back. For a moment she imagined that he was watching her.

Standing perfectly still, she waited, hoping she'd not woken him or the boys. She didn't need Mr. Barrington seeing just how awkward and clumsy she was this morning. Several seconds passed. He didn't move and soon, his deep even breathing filled the morning stillness. Relief washed over her. At least he wouldn't be hovering close waiting for her to fail.

Abby soon found a pile of wood in a metal wood-box and near it matches. Kindling in hand, she opened the small door at the base of the stove and laid the wood inside.

Her hands trembled with cold as she squatted before the small opening and lit the dried twigs with a match. Cupping her hand around the flame, she held it under her fragile pile of sticks and waited for the fire to catch.

Slowly the fire flickered to life. The dried wood cracked and popped. Gingerly, Abby laid larger pieces of wood on the fire, blowing gently until the flames burned bright.

She set back on her heels smiling. She'd started hundreds of stove fires in her life but none had given her more satisfaction.

Over the next hour, she encountered obstacle on top of obstacle. First it was venturing outside into the cold, tramping through the three inches of snow to the rain barrel and cracking through the layer of ice with her bucket to get water for coffee. Then it was sorting through the assortment of empty tins until she found the coffee and then the grinder. Then there was the matter of a clean mixing bowl. With none to be found, she was forced to wash one of the dirty wooden bowls stacked on the counter. It was caked with unrecognizable dough.

No matter which direction she turned there was a roadblock. This cabin, like Mr. Barrington, was daring her to quit.

Like a spoiled mistress, Montana was beautiful but exacting. But Abby was used to the spoiled and difficult.

Her only saving grace was that Mr. Barrington had slept through it all and not witnessed her struggles.

As Matthias lay on his back and listened to Miss Smyth move about the kitchen, he would have sworn a herd of Buffalo made less noise.

He'd awoken the instant she'd turned on her lantern, about four by his reckoning. He'd been surprised when she'd risen so early. Knowing the mess she faced, he half expected her to give up and go back to bed once she got a good look at it. But she hadn't gone back to bed. She'd continued to plow through the mess, banging her pots and pans as she worked.

To his surprise, as the first bits of morning sun seeped through the window, the delicious smell of freshly brewed coffee filled the cabin.

Matthias propped his hands under his head and looked into the kitchen. He expected to see Miss Smyth, standing tall. But in the deceptive morning light, he saw a woman, kneeling by the stove, her face turned in profile. And for just a moment, he imagined he saw Elise.

He sucked in a sharp breath and vaulted out of the bed. He'd worn his shirt and pants to bed, but the cold air burned through his clothing as he raked a trembling hand through his hair.

Startled, she turned. "You're awake."

The sound of her voice calmed him immediately, banishing the specters from the past. "Yeah."

Regaining his balance, he pulled on his boots and laced them up.

She brushed nervous hands on her apron—Elise's apron. "Good morning," she said. "I've made coffee."

Silent, he watched as she poured him a cup of hot coffee from the pot Elise had brought from Missouri.

Unreasonable irritation grated over his bones as he stepped toward the warm stove and reached for the cup she offered. His fingers brushed hers. The cup warmed his icy fingers. And despite his best intentions to remain aloof, his gaze held hers and a fizzle of energy shot through his body. Before Elise had gotten sick, their first mornings had been spent making love and it had taken all that was in him to leave her so that he could do his chores. He'd not allowed himself to think about those days for a long time and the fact that Abby's presence was fueling those memories churned his guilt.

Blushing under his gaze, she turned back to her sink. "The last thing I expected today was snow. It was so warm yesterday." Her tone sounded stilted, formal.

"Late spring storms happen, but I'd hoped that after the last few warm days we'd finally turned the corner," he said.

"Will it last long?"

The morning chill had added color to her cheeks and sunlight caught her hair, casting a honey-blond hue. "Hopefully not long."

"Do you have a lot to do today?"

"I've got to ride out and check the herds. A few calves were born a couple of weeks ago. I need to see how they fared."

He cradled the cup in his hand then sipped it. To his surprise it tasted good. Real good. Foolish but he was almost sorry for it. He wanted her to do something wrong—something to prove that she was better off leaving.

"I haven't sorted through the kitchen yet, so I won't be able to make you a hot breakfast but Frank left behind hard tack and I've sliced some ham."

How long had it been since he'd had a hot meal? "No matter."

"I wrapped them in a cloth for you to take to the range."

He frowned down at the bundle she pushed across the table toward him. More irritated, he swallowed the last of his coffee and scooped up the bundle. He'd not grow dependent on her. "I'd best get going."

She followed him to the door. "We'll see you this evening."

He shrugged on his guns and reached for his coat. "You won't have trouble with the boys?" He couldn't say why, but he didn't worry about leaving Tommy and Quinn with her. She'd do right by them.

She smiled. "We'll be fine."

No, today wouldn't be hard. The hard part would come later when she left. Sooner or later she'd realize how harsh this land could be and she'd leave. He resolved to have a talk with the boys. He didn't want them getting too attached to Miss Smyth.

She held out his hat, standing so close to him that he could feel the heat of her body. Her eyes sparked with a nervous anticipation. He'd always kissed Elise goodbye before he headed out to the range. Logic reminded him that he had hired Miss Smyth for the summer—nothing more, nothing less. And still, he wondered what it would feel like to kiss her, to hold her in his arms, and feel her body nestled close to his.

What would one kiss hurt? Just to touch her once. Abruptly he stopped the train of thought and took a step back.

"You look angry," she said. "Have I done something wrong?"

"No." Matthias shrugged on his coat. He

snatched his hat, jerked open the front door and closed it behind him.

Wind carried the brisk air across the valley churning the loosely packed snow. Tucking his head low, he headed toward the barn to milk the cow.

No matter what his body demanded, his brain understood that Miss Smyth was off limits.

Abby stared at the closed front door, wondering what she'd done wrong. She'd not expected anything from Mr. Barrington, but then his gaze had met hers. And instantly, she had seen the heat. Desire had seared her body. And she'd wanted to feel his lips against her.

But the fire in Mr. Barrington had vanished as quickly as hers had ignited. From the ashes, frustration and anger had risen.

She pressed the heel of her hand to her forehead. How had her life become such a complete mess so fast?

The fact that she wanted a man who didn't want her scared her more than the wilderness. Perhaps she should consider cutting her losses as he'd suggested all along and simply leave.

She shook her head. There was no going back to San Francisco. Her uncle would have discovered the missing money by now. He'd never have her arrested, fearing a scandal, but he would see to it that no one hired her if she returned.

Then again, she didn't have to return home. Chicago was less than a week's ride. And there was the east.

"Mommy!" Quinn's panicky voice sliced through her thoughts. He was still asleep, but thrashing wildly. Tommy slept next to him but it would be just a matter of seconds before he'd wake if she didn't quiet Quinn.

Abby hurried over to the bed, stumbling around a sack of flour in the process. She sat on the edge of the bed and patted the boy on the back. "It's all right, Quinn, Abby's here."

Her touch soothed the boy and soon he settled down. He put his thumb in his mouth and rolled onto his stomach.

Abby's heart squeezed as she saw the worry lines in the boy's face. She stroked the bangs off his forehead, studying the sprinkle of freckles there. His frown reminded her of Mr. Barrington, as did his nose. But his lighter coloring and pale blond hair were likely from his mother.

"Momma," he mumbled, his thumb still in his mouth.

She remembered those long nights after her own

mother had died. The loneliness had been crushing and there'd been no one to talk to, no one to dry her tears. Quinn was only four but his sadness was just as real.

She glanced over at Tommy, who slept on the edge of the other side of the bed. On his back, his mouth hung open. He was snoring. Tommy was so young. Likely, he barely remembered his mother.

But Quinn did remember. Leaning forward, she kissed him on the forehead. "It's all right, Quinn. I won't leave you."

The front door slammed closed.

She jumped to her feet and saw Mr. Barrington standing at the front door holding a bucket of milk. Snowflakes peppered his shoulders and hat. And his expression looked murderous.

"What's going on?" he said, his voice sharp.

She rose. "Quinn had a nightmare. He was calling for his mother," she whispered.

Mr. Barrington's features softened a fraction. "He's not had those in a while. Frank's leaving must have stirred up old dreams."

"He's back to sleep now. And if you keep your voice down he'll stay that way for another hour or two. I could use the quiet to get the dishes clean."

He strode into the kitchen and set the bucket down. He paused for a moment, then shoved out a breath and faced her. "Maybe it's best you leave as soon as the snow melts. It'll be a day or two at the most."

He was looking after his children. But so was she now.

She stared at him a long moment, then nodded toward the front door. "You forgot your lunch. You best get going. We both have a lot of work to do."

Mr. Barrington's eyes narrowed and for a moment she thought he'd argue. But he didn't. He turned and left. This time there was no hint of a kiss, no jolt of desire.

Abby doubted she'd ever worked so hard as she did this day. In San Francisco, her days had been filled with activity but there'd always been diversions to get her out of the kitchen. Back home, after breakfast was served, she had a quiet half hour to read and enjoy her breakfast. And the midmorning trips to the market were always time for gossip and conversation with the vendors.

But in Montana, the work never stopped. It took her nearly a half hour to scrub caked-on food from the skillet and bowls. As soon as the dishes were stacked neatly on the dish rack, she dug a few cakes of yeast and flour from the town supplies and made sourdough starter so that by week's end there'd be bread for the table. Next, it was time to strain the milk.

She'd just begun sorting the supplies when Quinn sat up in his bed and rubbed his eyes.

"I have to pee," he said.

Hearing his brother's voice Tommy sat up and yawned. "Me, too."

She thought about her own early-morning trip through the snow to the outhouse. She shivered. "Well, then, get your coats and boots on. There are a couple of inches of snow on the ground out there."

Quinn's eyes brightened. "Snow!" He scrambled out of bed and tugged on his well-worn boots.

Tommy quickly yanked on his boots and ran up to Abby. He thrust his foot toward her. "Tie me."

Abby knelt down. She pulled the shoe's tongue up straight and smoothed out his socks before she tied the shoelaces. His toes bumped against the tips of the shoes. He'd need new ones soon.

Both boys grabbed their jackets from the edge of the bed where Matthias had left them last night and hurried out the front door.

"Be careful out there!" Abby said, running after them as she shrugged on her own coat.

Laughing, they ran to the outhouse. Quinn scooped up a handful of snow and hurled it at

Tommy, hitting him squarely in the chest. Instead of crying, Tommy grabbed his own ball of snow and propelled it into Quinn's head.

"That's enough out of you two," she schooled. "You've no clean clothes and I don't want you getting wet."

The boys' laughter trailed through the clean morning air as they darted into the outhouse while Abby waited outside.

"Is everything all right in there?"

"Yessss," Quinn shouted.

When she didn't hear from Tommy, she knocked on the door. "Tommy?"

"My buttons are stuck."

Though she'd heard enough of Cook's bawdy stories, she had no firsthand knowledge of the male plumbing. She could unhook buttons, but Tommy was on his own from there.

"Come out here then," she said, opening the door. Quinn was just fastening his pants.

Tommy wiggled and shifted his feet from side to side. "Hurry."

She wrestled with the buttons. "If you'd stop wiggling, I would."

He held still for all of two or three seconds before he started wiggling again. Fortunately, this time she unhooked the buttons and scooted him back into the outhouse. ''Quinn, stay with your brother in case he needs assistance.''

''He can do it by himself. Pa showed him.''

She thought about Tommy's slender body falling into the outhouse hole. ''Well, just stay in there anyway.''

Quinn grumbled something about babies, then shouted, ''He's spraying the walls.''

''With what?'' Abby shouted.

Tommy giggled. So did Quinn.

Abby opened the door just as Tommy yanked up his pants. The smell of urine told her exactly what he'd been about. ''Thomas Barrington, come out here this instant.''

She knelt down and started to fasten his pants. ''No more spraying.''

The boys laughed.

Abby couldn't help but smile. She had not the faintest idea how to raise boys, but she imagined it would be an adventure.

She hustled the children back into the warm cabin and took off her coat. As she hung her coat on the peg by the door, Quinn and Tommy shrugged theirs off and dropped them on the floor.

''Oh, no, little misters. We'll be hanging our coats from now on.''

''But Pa doesn't care,'' Quinn said.

"I do."

He crossed his arms. "But you ain't our ma."

"That is correct, but you will hang your coats, nonetheless. And the correct word is aren't, not ain't." She moved a kitchen chair closer to the pegs. "Climb up now and hang those coats. We'll wash up for breakfast and then get to work on this place."

"Breakfast!" Tommy said. He scrambled up on the chair. "I'm hungry."

Quinn kept his lips flat and his expression defiant, but she saw the twinkle of excitement in his eyes.

After the boys washed their hands, she served them hard tack, ham and warmed milk. Neither complained about the simple fare and each asked for seconds.

Once the breakfast dishes were scraped and cleaned, they set about the task of sorting through the supplies from town.

When the downstairs was somewhat organized she climbed the ladder to her loft. The boys followed. Together they smoothed out the blankets.

"What's that?" Quinn said pointing to her bundle of possessions still bound in the tablecloth.

"It's just a few things I brought from home."

She unwrapped the tablecloth. As if they'd found

a buried treasure, the boys studied the meager contents. Quinn picked up a brush and Tommy studied her black Sunday shoes, which had long lost their sheen.

''What's that?'' Quinn said pointing to a package wrapped in pink tissue paper and bound with a delicate white ribbon.

That special extra purchase she'd bought when she'd arrived in Sacramento. It was a cotton nightgown trimmed with lace and bought special for her wedding night. Less than two weeks ago she'd watched the shopkeeper gently wrap the gown in the tissue paper. She'd imagined what it would feel like to have her husband unfasten the row of tiny pearls that trailed down the middle.

Then, her husband had no face. He'd simply been words on a page.

Now, he was a flesh-and-blood man, with rawboned features and penetrating blue eyes. This time she pictured Matthias's rough hands on the buttons and her naked flesh. A burning sensation flared in her body.

''It's nothing of import,'' she said, her voice rusty. She cleared her throat and set the bundle aside.

The gown, like her dreams, had no place in Montana.

Chapter Seven

By late afternoon the sun scorched through the clouds, revealing a vibrant blue sky. Under the warming sun, the snow thinned to reveal patches of green dotting the countryside.

Watching his herd of cattle, Matthias leaned forward in his saddle. His low-crowned Stetson blocked the bright sun from his eyes.

Last night's snowfall had been a few inches at most. If the warm temperatures held, it would be completely gone by tomorrow and his cattle would soon be grazing. This snowfall had been an annoyance, but not a disaster like the crushing blizzards of a year ago when he'd lost half his herd.

Those had been some of the darkest days of his life. As his cattle had died, he'd been trapped in the cabin with the boys and a wife who by then didn't have the strength to get out of bed. His life had been falling apart. He'd never felt more helpless, more out of control.

A sane man would have abandoned his land which had bled so much from him. Yet he had stayed. He'd never walked away from a fight and he hadn't walked away from this one.

And look what it had cost him.

Anger choked his throat.

He should still cut his losses and move back to Missouri. Frank had said there'd be a place for him if he returned. He hated the idea of returning east and never would have considered the move if his choices only involved him. But he had the boys to consider.

Back east, they could go to a real school, have friends of their own and not worry each winter if this one would be the one to finally crush their tiny family.

But the idea of returning to the city where a man could barely breathe stuck in Matthias's craw. And with the railroad scouts looking for cattle and horses, he was so close to making a fine profit.

He looked up at the cloudless sky. "I reckon you think I'm a fool, Elise. You were right when you said we should leave." He'd taken to talking to Elise when he was out on the range. If anyone were to see him, they'd think him a damn fool, but talking to her had helped keep him sane this last year.

The whisper of the wind in the trees was his only answer.

"I reckon you know by now I hired a woman to look after the boys. She seems good with them and she's got a kind heart. I'm certain she'll pick up stakes by the end of the summer. I remember how much you hated it out here."

He rubbed his forehead. He didn't dare voice his attraction to Miss Smyth. Speaking it aloud would make it all the more tangible. The more sinful. "She's only a hired hand," he said with a little too much emphasis. "I made a pledge to you never to love again."

It had been a promise he'd made as Elise lay dying. In those dark hours, he'd have bargained with the devil to save her. "And I'm going to keep my word."

Suddenly tired, he reined his horse around and started back to the cabin. He arrived an hour before sunset, but by the time he'd finished his chores in the barn, the sun had dipped behind the horizon. Orange-red light slashed across the land and the distant mountains. This was his favorite time of day. The fading sun set the land ablaze. The beauty of it always took his breath away. There were no views like this in Missouri.

As soon as his boot hit the front step, he heard the boys yelling, "Pa!" He smiled. As tired as he was, he liked hearing the excitement in their voices.

He reached for the front door just as it jerked open. The boys piled out onto the porch. Each was jumping up and down excitedly at the threshold. He squatted, not remembering the last time he'd seen them this lively.

Tommy swept his arms wide, proudly showcasing the cabin. "Look what we did today."

Quinn frowned, placing his small hand over Matthias's eyes. "No! No! First you close your eyes."

"We played games today!" Tommy said.

Matthias chuckled. "What kind of games?"

"We made laundry piles! And we put away boxes!"

Matthias nodded, marveling at the fact that Miss Smyth had turned chores into an adventure. "Miss Smyth's games."

"Yes," Quinn said. "Now keep your eyes closed and I will lead you inside."

Matthias complied, rising slowly as each boy took a hold of his hands.

"Don't peek, Pa," Tommy said.

"I'm not," he said. He moved into the main

room, half expecting to trip over one of the sacks or boxes he'd hauled in last night. "When are you going to let me see?"

"Now!" Quinn said.

Matthias opened his eyes, his gaze scanning the room. Not only had the bed been made but all the supplies had been put away. Laundry piles—one dark and one light—sat neatly in the corner. The wood floor had been swept clean and the dishes in the sink had been scrubbed and stacked on the shelves.

The smell of freshly baked beans and corn cakes greeted him. He'd not realized how hungry he was until this moment, and his mouth started to water.

A rustle of skirts and the clang of pots had his gaze swinging to the kitchen. There he saw Miss Smyth, still wearing Elise's blue-checkered apron, only now it was covered with smudges of cornmeal. Since this morning she'd coiled her braid into a tight knot at the base of her neck. To his surprise he preferred her braid loose, swinging seductively above her bottom.

She turned then and their gazes locked. As if reading his thoughts, color rose in her neck and cheeks as she looked at him. "Welcome home."

For the first time in his life, he felt awkward with a woman. Not a wife or a lover, yet more than just a servant. He cleared his throat. "Looks like you've been busy."

"There's been a lot to do." She lowered her gaze back to her pot on the stove. "Supper is ready if you're hungry."

"I could eat a bear."

Quinn frowned. "We don't have bear, Pa, only beans."

Matthias laughed. Lord, but it felt good to laugh. "Beans will be just fine."

"Well, have a seat at the table," she said. "I'll make you a plate."

He noticed then that the kitchen table had been cleaned. Napkins were folded and tucked under the forks and a plate of biscuits set in the center. The table looked inviting. He felt like a traitor for thinking it, but for the first time in a while he was glad to be home.

Miss Smyth stirred her pot. Her movements weren't as unsure as Elise's had been. Instead, she moved with efficient precision. Every action had a purpose. He couldn't imagine her sitting by the river reading poetry as Elise had or daydreaming about taking a steamer to Paris. Elise's gentility had been what had attracted him. She was the mirror opposite to his raw wild nature, coaxing him back from the wilderness with her soft words and tender smiles.

Miss Smyth was no-nonsense. She wasn't the kind of woman who cajoled. She ordered, a trait he was more than happy to see.

"How was your day, Mr. Barrington?" Her voice was cheery and she sounded genuinely interested.

"It was fine."

She wrapped a cloth around her hand and peeked in the oven at a skillet of cornbread. "I didn't know if you preferred biscuits or cornbread so I made both."

"I like both," he said, stunned at her efficiency.

"Did you find your herd?"

"They were right where I left them. The storm didn't do as much damage as I feared. I accounted for all the calves."

"I've a good bit to learn about ranching."

He rubbed the back of his neck with his hand. "Hard work and luck is all a man needs to succeed."

"I suspect you are a hard worker." She inserted a knife in the cornbread. Satisfied when it came out clean, she removed the pan from the oven.

"It's the luck I lack."

She smiled, looking at him. "Well, perhaps that has changed."

He found himself relaxing, and then caught himself. Perhaps because he'd not had anyone ask him about his day in so long. This easy conversation made him feel just a little too married. "I've learned not to count on anything."

"You men wash up," she said, her smile a little less relaxed. "Dinner's ready."

"We got to wash our hands *again?*" Quinn said. "But we washed before breakfast and lunch. Ain't we clean enough?"

"*Aren't* we clean enough," Miss Smyth corrected.

"They had a bath recently," Matthias said.

"They've been rummaging around on the floor since lunchtime." She nodded toward the sink. "There's water in the basin and a rag to wash."

The three washed, but none was happy about it, including Matthias.

"I like Abby," Quinn said.

"Is she going to be our new mother?" Tommy said.

Matthias pulled in a deep breath. "She's just helping me out for the summer."

"She acts like a mother," Tommy said.

Quinn wiped his damp hands on his pants. "Tommy called her ma twice today."

Tommy looked up at his father, clearly unsure.

Matthias swallowed the jolt of anger. "It's okay, son."

Tommy looked relieved and they headed back to the table.

However, despite his words, Matthias's anger spread like wildfire in August. It made no sense to him. The boys had asked fair questions, and it wasn't Tommy's fault that he'd called Miss Smyth "Ma." But it did bother him that Miss Smyth had slipped into Elise's role so easily. And what added salt to the wound was that Miss Smyth was doing a better job than Elise.

When they sat at the table, Miss Smyth set a pot of hot beans on the table. It had been a long time since he'd eaten a hot meal in his house and even though he knew it was rude he didn't thank Miss Smyth. Instead, he fell on the food. He served a plateful to each boy as they grabbed corncakes off the tin platter. Without a word exchanged between the three, they dug in.

Several minutes passed before he realized Miss Smyth wasn't eating. She sat primly in her seat, her hands folded in front of her, staring at them as if they'd grown horns.

Matthias set his fork down. It clanged against the plate a little too loudly. He was itching for a fight, if only to prove that he wasn't all that impressed with what Miss Smyth had done here today. "Something wrong?"

"It's customary to say prayers before a meal." Her voice sounded so damn reasonable. She snapped open her napkin and spread it over her lap.

He scowled. "We have never bothered with such formalities out here." In truth, they had when Elise had been healthy, but that had been so long ago.

Her chin lifted a notch at his stare, which had sent grown men running for cover. "Perhaps it's time you started."

His temper strained against good sense. "I don't see why."

"Don't you want better for the boys? Don't you want to see them grow up to be gentlemen who can move in polite circles?"

Deep inside, he saw the reason behind her words, but the burr under his skin wouldn't let him walk away. "Lady, the cows on the range and the trail bosses don't care if the boys know a bunch of useless society nonsense. *All* I care about is that they grow up to be honest and hard-working men."

She met his fiery gaze. "And those are important traits, but it's also important that they know their manners. One day they will go to school, perhaps a university, and they need to know how to handle themselves.''

He wasn't accustomed to a woman being so direct. When Elise had gotten angry there'd been tense silences and sighs. ''They're my boys, so what I say goes.''

''If I am to care for them—''

''You aren't their mother.'' He spoke much more sharply than he'd intended.

Miss Smyth's skin paled. Fire flashed in her eyes. She laid her napkin on the table. ''You're quite right, Mr. Barrington.'' She looked as if she'd say something else. But she realized the children had stopped eating and were starting intently at her.

Slowly, she rose. ''I'm going out for some fresh air.''

''This isn't the city. It's not wise to go roaming at night.''

She moved toward the front door, where her coat hung on a peg next to the children's. ''I've no intention of roaming.''

Tossing his napkin on the table, he rose. He'd been an ass and he knew it. ''You don't know your way around out there.'' He knew she was mad at him and frankly he couldn't blame her. She'd worked hard today and he'd been little more than a clod. It wasn't her fault that she wasn't Elise. Or that she never would be. ''If it's the outhouse that you're needing, I'll get my gun and go with you. There are bears this time of year.''

She reached for the door handle and opened it. ''I'd rather deal with a bear.''

Before he could say another word, she slammed the door behind her.

Tears stung Abby's eyes as she strode toward the barn. With no lantern, she had only the light from the half moon to guide her over the snow path Mr. Barrington had beaten between the house and the barn. She wasn't sure what she was going to do when she got to the barn. She simply knew she had to get out of the house.

She stumbled on an unseen stick and it took several quick awkward steps before she caught herself. In the city there was always a street lamp or lantern to guide the way. But out here the night was so blasted dark.

She wanted to hide from Mr. Barrington's unexplainable irritation and the shocked expressions on the boys' faces. She'd worked so hard today because she'd desperately wanted to make that cabin feel more like a home.

And Mr. Barrington, for reasons she'd never understand, had been annoyed with her for doing just that.

Reaching the barn, Abby pushed back the wooden latch that kept the door closed. Earlier, she and the boys had toured the homestead. She'd inspected the chicken house where she'd collected half a dozen eggs. As the boys chatted happily, she'd toured the barn, which unlike the house was surprisingly organized.

She paused inside the barn. The earthy smell of hay drifted over the chilly night air.

The interior was pitch-black and she could barely see her outstretched hand. Relying on the bits of moonlight by the door, she found a lantern hanging by the door and a box of matches. She lit the wick and turned it up until the light burned bright.

The barn had four stalls. Two sat empty. However, one stall on the north side held a chestnut gelding and on the other side there was a black mare with her colt.

Abby moved toward the mare and her colt. She held up the lantern. The mare eyed her with big brown eyes, then moved forward an inch as if to shield her baby.

"Don't worry, girl. I won't hurt your baby." Abby held out her flat palm, waiting for the horse to sniff her hand.

The horse snorted and did not approach. "Do you have a problem with me, too?" Despite the animal's haughtiness, she continued to hold out her hand. If anything, Miss Smyth was good at being patient. She'd spent the last ten years being nothing but patient.

A full minute passed before the horse sniffed, as if trying to figure out if Miss Smyth had a treat in her hand.

"Sorry, it's just me tonight."

The animal pawed at the dirt and turned her back, clearly uninterested in Abby.

Even the animals on the ranch seemed to have no need of her company.

She wasn't sure how long she stood there, watching the mare and her colt. The creak of the barn door opening had her turning.

Mr. Barrington stood in the doorway. Abby turned back to the horse.

"You going to stay out here all night?" Mr. Barrington's deep rich voice echoed in the barn.

Her stomach tightened and her skin grew hot. "Maybe. I like it out here. It's peaceful."

He strode up to the stall. When he stood next to her she realized just how tall he was. Abby had been taller than a good many men in her family, but Mr. Barrington stood at least five inches taller.

So close his shoulder nearly brushed hers. His masculine scent, a mixture of sweat and fresh air, spun around her. Annoyed by her reaction to him, she tightened her fingers into fists. She'd have left, but where would she go? Back to her loft where she could lie awake listening to him move about the cabin?

Neither spoke as he held out his hand to the mare. The animal approached instantly.

Stupid to feel a stab of jealousy over a horse, but she did. Every square inch of the homestead from the roughly hewn logs of the house, to the split-rail fences of the corral bore Mr. Barrington's mark. Elise's presence was all over the house and yard as well. Today, she'd wanted to make her mark, if only a small one, on the ranch.

"I put the boys to bed."

"Thank you." She'd imagined she'd be the one putting them down—saying their prayers, giving them a kiss good-night as she tucked the covers under their chins. *Dreams.* There she went again letting her dreams set her up for sadness.

"Temperature is going to drop off quickly," he said.

She'd never been good at small talk or ignoring a problem when it was staring her right in the face. "What does the temperature have to do with the fact that you were rude to me just now in front of the boys?''

He stared at her, no apology in his gaze. ''This situation is awkward.''

She tipped back her head, hysterical laughter bubbling inside her. ''I've never heard a greater understatement spoken, Mr. Barrington.''

''You're very direct,'' he said. His voice was as hard as his gaze.

''So I've been told.'' Her forthright manner had gotten her in trouble with her uncle and aunt more than once.

''I can take you back to town.''

A bitter smile twisted her lips. ''I didn't come this far for a twenty-four-hour stay on a ranch. I came out here to marry you.''

He tightened his fingers on the stall doors until the faint sound of wood cracking had him loosening his hold. ''A lie brought you here, not me. And the truth is, I'd make you or any woman a lousy husband. Loving Elise—'' He paused as if just mentioning her name hurt. ''Well, loving her used up all the love that was in me. There's just none left.''

The admission had cost him and as much as it hurt to hear his words, she appreciated his honesty.

Her aunt and uncle hadn't loved her. She supposed loving Joanne had used up all their love as well. Then there'd been Douglas. He'd had a fiancée back east. "I have a talent for attaching myself to people who can't love."

His eyes narrowed a fraction. "You've been married before?"

"No." Her penchant for honesty grated her own nerves. She wasn't interested in talking about her past, especially Douglas. "Just a family who didn't quite know what to do with me."

A slight breeze blew through the open door, teasing his thick black hair. She inhaled the scent of leather and fresh air.

He was a powerful man, who commanded the space he occupied. No wonder she felt a tug when he was close.

She wished she had a bag full of eloquent words that could magically make his pain and hers go away. Instead, she spoke plainly as she always did. "Elise is gone, Mr. Barrington, and for your sake and the boys, I am sorry."

His folded his arms over his chest, his face a rigid mask.

She should have taken his expression as warning that he didn't want to hear what she had to say. She didn't. "But the fact remains, until your herd brings in enough money to pay my return ticket, we are bound together. So how do you propose we make the best of it?"

Chapter Eight

"We don't," Mr. Barrington snapped.

His eyes blazed with anger and she could see he was spoiling for a fight.

Abby folded her arms over her chest but instead of getting angry, she switched tactics. Drawing in a breath, she forced her taut muscles to relax.

"Tell me about your wife," she said boldly. This was a risk. Elise's death was a raw wound that had not healed. But to save her future she had to understand his past.

Stiffening, he lowered his dark brows. "She's dead and buried—gone—and I don't like to talk about her."

Only feet separated them but it might have well have been a million miles. "I saw traces of her all over the cabin. Like it or not, she is still very present."

His jaw clenched so tightly a muscle spasmed in his cheek. "She is gone!"

"No, she's not. The aprons, curtains, the hash marks on the walls showing how tall Quinn was on his second birthday and Tommy on his first."

Mr. Barrington swallowed as a ghost of a smile touched his lips. "Quinn was standing on his toes that day. No matter how hard Elise tried to coax him into standing flat-footed, he wouldn't."

"I see the comment marks she made in her cookbook and the batter stains on the zucchini bread page."

His muscles were bunched so tight they looked ready to snap. "She wasn't a natural cook. But she was trying to learn. She wanted to please me."

Abby wanted to take his hand in hers as comfort, but didn't dare, certain he'd recoil. "Is that why she followed you out here?"

He drew in a deep breath and expelled it. "It was my idea to move west."

"Why?"

"The war devastated the south and for those who fought against the Union the bitterness was too great."

"Did you meet her in Missouri?"

"Yes, Elise grew up in St. Louis. After the war I made my way west. I'd been a sharpshooter in the rebel army. After the war, I discovered that there was a market for men like me out west. For ten years, I made my money bounty hunting. Six years ago, I tracked down a bank robber and drug him back to St. Louis for trial. This fella was well known and when I dropped him at the jailhouse word spread fast and a crowd gathered. Elise was in the crowd.'' He closed his eyes, as if summoning the moment. ''She wore a blue bonnet that day. I knew the minute I saw her we'd marry one day.''

Abby felt a stab of jealousy. She'd never been swept off her feet. ''And then you moved west.''

Her voice brought him back from the past. ''I wanted a place of our own. After my years out west, St. Louis was too crowded for me. I'd been to Montana a couple of times and loved it. I figured it would be the perfect place for us to start our new life.''

''Did Elise like it?''

His expression reflected sadness. ''We arrived in the spring. It was an unusually warm spring in '74. The first few days were like a great adventure. We camped in a tent while I began to build our cabin. But as the days turned to weeks, her excitement soured. She never complained but I knew. And then late that summer she got pregnant with Quinn. She was sick a lot those first few months.'' He shook his head. "I should have pulled us out then. But after Quinn's birth we were in our cabin and her health rallied."

"How did she die?"

"Pregnancy was hard on her. It took a lot out of her carrying Tommy. But again she rallied. I didn't want any more children after Tommy was born, but Elise had other ideas. She wanted a girl. From the moment she got pregnant the third time it was a disaster. She was so sick that winter she couldn't lift her head off the pillow. I sent for Frank and he came in the early spring. A week after Frank arrived, she went into labor. The baby was a girl, but too early, too small. Elise never recovered from the birthing. She died the next day."

His story broke her heart. Unexpected death could rip lives apart. Her parents' deaths had changed her forever. "Montana had nothing to do with her death."

He shook his head. "She hated this place."

"She couldn't have hated it that much or there wouldn't be so many personal touches around the cabin. A woman who hates a place doesn't make curtains for it."

He stabbed his fingers through his hair. "She missed the city."

"Missing one place doesn't mean you hate another."

Lantern light shadowed the high slash of his cheekbones. He looked at her, his blue eyes almost black with anger born in sadness. "We've talked enough for one night."

Abby knew she'd pushed him. Though there were a thousand other questions to ask, she knew they'd made a start tonight. And she understood she'd have more luck carving granite with a butter knife than getting him to say another word.

"It is getting late. And it's been a long day," she agreed.

Lifting her lantern, she moved past him to the barn door. He trailed silently behind her, closing the barn door after they stepped out into the cold night air.

"That lantern stays with the barn." Without waiting for her response, he took the lantern from her. He blew out the flame and hung it from the peg by the door.

Without the small flickering flame, the night seemed to swallow them up. Clouds had drifted in front of the moon, and she could barely see a foot in front of her. "Then how do you propose we find our way back?"

"I know every root and gulch on my property."

"I can't say the same."

Strong fingers captured her elbow. "Don't worry, I'm right behind you."

The warmth of his fingers against hers sent shock waves up her arm. Her mind drifted and for a moment she imagined those same hands caressing the underside of her jaw, unbuttoning her blouse, and touching her naked skin.

Shaking off the image, Abby lifted her skirts and started toward the house, taking one careful step at a time. Icy snow crunched under her feet seconds before she slipped. She fell back hard and would have hit the ground if Mr. Barrington hadn't had a hold of her.

The ice made regaining her footing all the more difficult. Instinct had her grabbing onto his coat lapels and pulling herself upright. She found herself facing his dimpled chin, her knuckles pressing against his muscled chest. Their lips were only inches apart.

His heart hammered in his chest against her hand. Warm breath brushed her cheek as he angled his face forward a fraction. Desire pulsed in her veins.

Before she thought, she rose up on tiptoe and gripped his sleeves with quivering fingers. Her heart raced and without a thought to propriety, she pressed her lips to his. Her closemouthed kiss was chaste by any standards and she felt awkward as he stood as rigid as a stone, staring down at her with eyes as black as Satan's. Suddenly, she felt foolish. She scrambled for an apology.

She didn't need one.

His strong arm banded around her narrow waist and he pulled her against his chest, his arousal pressing into her thigh.

For Matthias, Abby's chaste kiss was like a spark to dry tinder. Desire flamed in him, scorching his veins with a white-hot need. He gave no thought to the past or the future but only to satisfying a lust thrumming in his veins—the lust he thought had died.

In the pale moonlight, he saw surprise flicker in Abby's eyes as she looked up at him. She'd never been properly kissed, and he thought for an instant that he'd frightened her and that she'd go stumbling back to the cabin to the safety of her loft. In truth, it would be best for them both.

Instead, she leaned forward, pressing her full breasts against his chest.

As if his body had a will of its own, Matthias slid his hand up her back and cupped her neck in his hand. Fisting a handful of hair, he tugged her head back. Their warm breaths mingled in the chilled night.

The cold night air forgotten, he kissed her on the mouth fully. Moaning, she wrapped her arms around his neck. The fire in his veins burned hotter.

He slid his tongue into her mouth. He explored, demanded, possessed. She tasted as sweet as honey and he was ready to devour her here and now.

She moaned softly as he lowered his hand to her breast and circled the nipple until it formed a hard peak.

He trailed kisses down from her lips to the hollow of her neck. "God help me, but I want you."

She arched back, moistening her lips with her tongue. "Yes."

He stared down at her pale face in the dim moonlight. Her breasts pushed against his chest with each ragged breath of hers. Her thighs quivered. White-hot lust surged in his veins and loins.

Consequences be damned. He'd take her back to the barn and on a fresh mound of hay make love to her. His need had grown wild, tormented by too many long nights without a woman.

He kissed her again, nibbling her bottom lip with his teeth as he cupped her full round breast. Frustrated by the fabric that separated him from her bare flesh, he bunched the fabric in his hand, ready to tear it.

The front door to the cabin opened with a bang. "Pa, are you out there?" Quinn's voice skidded through the night and struck him like a cold blast of air.

As if he'd been doused with a bucket of ice water, he broke the kiss. Still holding Abby, he stared down at her. Her hair was tousled, her lips swollen and her eyes misty with desire from his kiss.

"What the hell are we doing," he said, his words scraping over his vocal cords.

She blinked, pressing her fingertips to her lips. The clouds faded from her eyes. "I wouldn't think it needed explanation."

Releasing her, he shoved his fingers through his hair.

"Pa!" Quinn shouted louder.

"I'll be right there, Quinn. Shut the door so you don't let the heat out."

"Are you coming in soon?"

"Yes, just close the door, son."

"Okay, Pa."

When the door slammed shut, Matthias tried to collect the shattered pieces of his composure. His erection still throbbed, a painful reminder of what had almost happened. "I'm sorry."

Sadness and frustration collided in her eyes. "I'm not."

"We shouldn't have done that," he rasped.

"It's not a sin to live again."

In the year since Elise had died he'd lived in limbo. Each day he'd not concentrated on anything more than his boys and just getting through the day. Now in the blink of an eye, he had another woman living under his roof stirring desires so strong they rivaled what he'd felt for Elise.

He'd not done anything wrong, but he couldn't shake the gnawing guilt in his gut.

He shoved shaky fingers through his hair. Reality and painful memories cooled the remains of his desire. The night's chill seeped into his bones. "It's time we got inside."

"So that's it?" Her hackles rose and she stiffened. "Don't you want to talk about what just happened?"

He tightened his jaw so hard he imagined he heard teeth snapping. "No."

A week later, the sun had warmed the land, banishing the chill. Abby wished it could also melt the chill that had settled between Mr. Barrington and her.

The kiss had shocked them both. For her, she'd

not expected her knees to weaken when he'd touched her. She'd not expected her senses to swim when she felt the hunger in his bunched muscles. She'd not expected to *want* so much.

He'd clearly not anticipated his attraction to her, either. His reaction had angered him. Though he'd not said as much, since that night he'd been overly formal and had kept his distance. Clearly, he'd not wanted to feel anything for her. But he had.

Despite Mr. Barrington's silence, each time he entered the cabin no matter if she were cooking in the kitchen or lying in her bed at night in the loft, she was aware of him.

His presence filled the cabin. Dominated it. And with each passing day the restlessness she'd felt when he'd kissed her had grown.

Abby punched down the bread dough and sprinkled flour on it. She glanced up out the window and watched the boys playing pick-up sticks, a game she'd fashioned for them out of twigs.

"The stage is coming!" Quinn shouted from the front porch.

Abby looked up from her bread dough out the kitchen window. In the distance the stage, surrounded by a plume of dust, rumbled toward the cabin. She recognized Holden's coach immediately. "Now what the devil is he doing here?"

Curiosity quickly gave way to excitement at the idea of having a guest. She enjoyed the boys but, after a week living with children and a very silent Mr. Barrington, she welcomed the idea of talking to another person.

She quickly shaped the loaves and set them by the window to rise. Wiping her hands, she moved out onto the front porch next to the boys who both were jumping up and down.

"Mr. McGowan is coming, Abby," Tommy said.

Abby smiled. "I can see that. What do you think brings him out here?"

"Horses," Quinn said.

"Horses?"

"Pa trades the tired ones for fresh ones," Quinn said.

"I didn't know your pa's house was a stagecoach stop."

"People never stay long," Quinn said. "They don't think Pa is friendly."

Imagine that.

The stage rolled to a stop in the yard by the corral. Holden set the brake and tied off the reins. He touched the brim of his hat. "I reckon it's Mrs. Barrington now."

She lifted an eyebrow, unwilling to show any

signs that her life was tipped out of balance. "No, sir, the name is still Smyth."

Surprise flickered and then he climbed down from the driver's seat and strode over to the boys. The sun had deepened his skin to a dark brown and the trail had coated his clothes with a fine layer of dust. With the boys so close he guarded his words carefully. "Did I hear right? The name is still *Smyth?*"

She glanced down at the boys who stared up at Holden with grinning faces. "Yes."

Holden scratched his head. "I reckon he was M-A-D." He spelled the word so the boys wouldn't get the meaning of their conversation.

She wasn't ready to let this man, who'd been a party to the deception, off the hook so easily. "Oh, yes."

He paled a fraction. "I reckon he'll want to have a chat with me."

"I'm sure he would, but you're in luck, he usually doesn't come in until quite late."

Holden glanced over his shoulder. "I saw Matthias on the trail. He'll be coming up presently."

The skin on the back of her neck tingled. She'd not seen Matthias before sunset in over a week. And the idea excited her. She refused to think about how she'd lain awake these last few nights, trying to erase the feel of his hands and lips on her body. "I'm sure he's got a few choice words."

"Look, Miss Smyth," he said, glancing at the boys. "I am sorry if this isn't working out for you." The man looked truly distressed and she found it hard to hold on to her anger. "Everybody knows Matthias needs a W-I-F-E and well, you seemed perfect for him."

"Time will tell."

His eyes brightened with anticipation. "So it isn't a lost cause between you two."

She thought about the kiss. "Not completely."

His face split into a wide grin. "Good." He reached in his pocket and pulled out two pieces of licorice. "Mind if I give them to the boys?"

Quinn and Tommy's smiles were radiant. "Please, please," they shouted.

"Of course," she said, unable to deny them the rare treat. Before either could bite into the candy she added, "And what do you say?"

"Thank you."

The boys hurried off toward a tall poplar tree that often served as their special fort. It gave them some privacy, but it was close enough for her to keep an eye on them from the kitchen window.

"Looks like you might be taming those young fellows," Holden said.

Her heart warmed as she looked past him and watched Quinn and Tommy comparing their candies. No doubt they were checking to see who had gotten the biggest piece. "They're good boys."

"That they are."

She should be mad at him for the part he had played in this deception. But the truth was that despite the mess of this situation, she'd never felt more alive than she had in the last week. "I should have Mr. Barrington shoot you."

He grimaced. "He may well do that, anyway."

She shook her head. "Well, then I best feed you supper first. Can you stay? I've a stew on and bread in the oven."

He grinned, his white even teeth contrasting with his dark skin. "I'd be obliged. It's been a good while since I had a hot home-cooked meal."

The idea of company buoyed her sprits. She'd cleaned her grandmother's tablecloth but with two young children and Matthias to feed, she'd not bothered to set the table with it yet.

"You have any passengers?" It would be nice to see another woman.

"Not this time. Just hauling parcels and supplies for the railroad this time. But rail companies looking to put lines in, I'm willing to bet I'll be hauling a good many scouts and surveyors sooner than later.''

''Well, if you ever need to stop, you're welcome any time. I've always enjoyed cooking for a crowd.''

He nodded, staring at her with a more serious eye. ''I'd be willing to take you up on that. Matthias is always good for fresh horses—has the best stock in the valley—but he or Frank weren't much for cooking or welcoming strangers. We always stayed just long enough to change our horses.''

She remembered her very long ride into town. ''The day I arrived we didn't stop here.''

He rubbed his chin, ducking his head. ''I thought it best we take a different route that day. Seemed only fair to you that you meet Matthias in town. Just in case.''

She lifted an eyebrow. ''Just in case he sent me packing?''

''He can dig his heels in when he don't want to do something.''

''Yes, I've learned that about him.''

''Well, he must like you, because he doesn't waste a moment on people he doesn't like.''

''For now our arrangement is strictly business. I'm broke and he needs a housekeeper. After his roundup, he pays me twenty-five dollars and then I can buy a ticket to someplace else. You and Mrs. Clements and the others have backed him into a neat little corner.''   .

Holden laughed. ''Nobody ever backs Matthias Barrington into a corner. The man does what he pleases. If he didn't want you here, you wouldn't be here.''

If he weren't a guest or if she knew him better, she'd have pressed him for more details. Instead she nodded toward the house. ''Come inside. Sit. I made a pie this morning.''

Pulling off his hat, Holden followed her into the cabin. He glanced around, amazed. ''I wouldn't have recognized the place.''

In the last week, she'd mended the laundry, dusted every piece of furniture and swept the floor. ''It took some doing to put the place into order.''

She sliced a piece of sweet potato pie and poured a glass of milk, setting both on the table in front of him. Before she sat, she took a quick glance out the window toward the boys. Licorice cords in their mouths, they were lying on their backs, staring at the clouds, their feet propped up on the tree.

She handed him a fork. ''Please eat up. You must be starved after the long ride from Butte.''

He dug into the pie. ''I swear if I had to dip another piece of hard tack into a plate of beans, I'm sure I'd go crazy.'' He put the piece of pie in his mouth. He closed his eyes and for a moment seemed lost in ecstasy. ''Ma'am, if the rest of your cooking tastes as good as this, I'll be stopping by regularly with passengers.''

The idea of seeing people regularly made her smile. She enjoyed the boys but sorely missed adult conversation. ''Guests are always welcome.''

He wiped crumbs from his mouth with a napkin. ''Well, you just make sure you charge them for your services.''

''Charge?''

He ate another piece of pie. ''Yes, ma'am. A dollar a meal.''

She laughed. ''That's outrageous. I could buy three meals for that in San Francisco.''

''This isn't the city. Not to men who've not had a decent meal or a woman's touch in their lives in months.'' He ate another bite of pie. ''Miss Smyth, you're going to make a fortune.''

Mr. Barrington's purposeful footsteps sounded on the front porch and in the next instant his large frame blocked the front door. The top four buttons of his shirt were open, revealing chest hair curling with sweat. The sight of him made her heart miss a beat.

And she'd have smiled a greeting if he didn't look angry enough to spit nails. "Holden, you got to the count of three to get out of my house before I shoot you."

Chapter Nine

Murderous thoughts shot through Matthias when he'd first seen Holden's carriage ride over the horizon. He and Abby were in this mess together because of his friend's meddling. But when he'd strode onto his own front porch and heard the laughter and joy in Abby's laugh, anger turned to jealousy.

In the week she'd been here, he'd seen her smile at the boys but he'd not heard her laugh. Her laughter rang as sweet as church bells, filling the cabin with life.

Though he'd done his best to keep his distance, he still noted the changes she conjured each day. Abby had filled the lifeless cabin with an energy it had never possessed. No longer a solemn place he dreaded returning to each night.

All were good reasons, in his mind, to keep his distance. He didn't want to need her. Add to that the attraction that sizzled in his veins each time he saw her, and he had an explosive mix that was sure to blow up in his face sooner or later.

But he'd vowed to keep his hands to himself. His arrangement with Abby was temporary. And he'd be damned before he let lust or loneliness bind her to this harsh and fickle land.

Holden was a good man—they'd been friends of five years and he'd helped him through the darkest days after Elise's death. But Abby wasn't right for him.

As Matthias shoved through his front door he noticed Abby first. She sat at the table across from Holden, her eyes sparkling with laughter, her hair in a long braid that draped between her full breasts. The sun had lightened her hair and added color to her cheeks, making her look almost radiant. Damn, but he could feel himself growing hard just looking at her.

Color rose in her cheeks as if she could read his thoughts. "You're home early, Mr. Barrington."

He cleared his throat. "I saw the stage."

With a great effort, he tore his gaze from Abby and settled it on Holden. He had to remind himself he was angry with his old friend. "If you had any good sense, you'd stay clear of my property after what you and Mrs. Clements did.''

Holden, who sat in his chair at the dinner table, glanced up from his half-eaten piece of pie. ''I figured if you hadn't cooled off after a week you'd never cool off. Plus I wanted to make sure Miss Abby was faring well.''

''She's doing just fine.''

Holden rose and thrust out his hand. ''So I can see. Though I don't know how she could be, stuck out here with a sour-faced man like you. You look like you could eat nails.''

''I just might before it's all over.'' Matthias hesitated, then took Holden's hand. ''Stop feeding my boys candy. Their teeth are going to rot out of their heads.''

Holden laughed. ''Ah, leave 'em be. Isn't often a boy gets to chew on a stick of licorice and stare at the clouds with his brother. And the boys look fitter than I've seen 'em in months.''

Matthias had Abby to thank for that. ''So what brings you this way? You don't waste daylight unless there's a reason.''

Holden nodded, the laughter fading from his eyes. ''A couple of reasons. A friend of mine in Butte said a representative from the rail is coming through town around early July. He's looking for horses—lots of 'em. You met him last week. Name is Stokes.''

Matthias remembered the dandy. "How many horses?''

"As many as he can get.''

Matthias hadn't rounded up his stock yet this year. There'd simply been no time. But with the railroad man coming to town and Abby watching the boys, he could do it. He'd have to work extra hard and fast, but if he pulled this one off, he could earn hard cash. "I can have three dozen for him by August.''

Holden nodded. "I'll pass it on to him. I already told him your horses are the best stock in the valley.''

Matthias nodded. For the first time in months the weight pressing on his shoulders eased. Suddenly, he felt like eating a piece of Abby's pie. "You said there were two reasons you came.''

"I came to talk to you about a little business proposition.''

Matthias lifted an eyebrow. "More business.''

Holden shrugged. "The valley is booming.''

"I'll pour a cup of coffee,'' Abby said.

"Thank you.'' He sat down at the table, noting its surface was smooth and clean, not sticky with grease and dirt. Last night when he'd slipped into bed, he noted the sheets were clean and smelled of fresh air and not stale smoke.

Abby set the coffee in front of him along with a slice of pie. "Company in the afternoon—I'd swear it was a holiday."

Matthias stared at the pie, astonished she'd baked the small miracle. He took a bite. "This is delicious."

Abby smiled. "I'm glad you like it."

Holden took another bite. "Where'd you learn to cook?"

Abby smiled. "At first I learned from my mother. Then later Cook."

Again Matthias was amazed how her face transformed when she grinned.

"Who's this Mrs. Cook?" Holden said.

"Cook isn't her name, it's her job. Her real name is Cora O'Neil. She is the cook in my aunt and uncle's house. She is a difficult woman but very talented. She taught me the finer points of baking."

The surprise on Holden's face mirrored what Matthias felt.

Holden scratched his head. "Your aunt and uncle have folks working for them? Must be pretty rich."

She shrugged. "They employ a butler, three maids and a gardener. My aunt would like to hire more but my uncle's income won't allow it."

"If you had all that, then what brought you out here?" Holden said.

Her smile vanished. "I simply wanted a change."

Matthias sensed a shift in her mood immediately. Her life in San Francisco hadn't been happy. She'd once said there'd be no going back to the city. Now he wondered why.

"That's one mighty big change," Holden said.

Matthias traced the rim of his cup with his calloused thumb. "If you were living in a house with servants, what were you doing working in the kitchen?"

Abby clasped her hands neatly in front of her on the table. "My uncle expected me to carry my own weight around the house."

"So you worked in his kitchens?" Matthias couldn't hide the bitterness in his voice.

The tension around her eyes that had been present when she'd arrived a week ago returned. "I wanted to work in the kitchen. It gave me something to do. I'm not one for idle pastimes."

The kitchen was a place to hide.

The people who came to Montana came to start over, often to get away from a past that wasn't pleasant. For him it had been the war.

He clamped down on any questions. She was

good to his boys and that's all he needed to know. The less he knew about her the easier it would be in the end when she left.

He pushed his half-eaten piece of pie away. "Holden, what's this business proposition you were talking about?"

"Well, you know how I come this way with the stage from time to time."

"We trade horses."

"Right, well, with the rail line coming in, I'll be doubling the number of times I make my route to accommodate the railroad men. Seeing as you have a woman on the ranch again, I figured when I stop my passengers could get out and stretch their legs, maybe get a meal if Abby is willing to cook. It'll mean more money."

Abby. When had Holden started calling her *Abby?*

Holden had proposed the same idea three years ago. Elise had been all for it at first, but she quickly found the extra work too demanding. She'd never complained but he saw how the extra work had drained her and so he'd gone to Holden and asked him to alter his route. "My days already feel like they are ten hours too short, anyway," he said more gruffly than he intended.

"I think it's a wonderful idea!" Abby said. "If

you give me an idea of what days you might be coming through then I could make extra that morning.''

Matthias tapped his index finger on the table. ''You've got your hands full as it is.''

Her eyes lighted with excitement. ''I've cooked dinner for fifty before. It takes planning but it's not impossible.''

He met her gaze. ''It's more work than you realize. I won't allow it.''

Abby's excitement turned to annoyance. Though she didn't move a muscle, she dug in her heels. ''You won't *allow* it.''

He could be stubborn, too. ''You heard me.''

Holden, sensing the shift, rose. ''I believe I best go check on the boys. You never know what those two might get into.'' He rose quickly and went outside before either of them could respond.

Matthias shoved out a hard breath. ''I don't want you taking on the extra work.''

''Frankly, I'd love the company and the extra money would be welcome. There'd be enough money to pay off your credit at the store and then some, I'll wager.''

The fact that he carried debt at the store still galled him. Until this spring, he'd always paid as he'd gone. ''I'll make it without any help.''

She arched an eyebrow. "You mean from me?"

He ground his teeth. "From anyone."

Her face paled with anger. "So we're back to that again?"

"What?"

"Me leaving."

He shrugged. "It's not a matter of *if* you leave, it's a matter of *when*."

She planted her hands on her hips. "I wish she was here."

"Who?"

"Elise. Then you could take a good long look at both of us, and you could see with your own two eyes that I am not her."

Rage roiled inside of him. "I know who you are."

"Do you? Every evening when you come home you look surprised to see me, as if you expect me to be gone."

Her words struck a nerve. She was right. He did expect her to vanish. And what was worse, that damn worry had taken root and grew every day.

"What's it going to take to prove to you that I'm not going anywhere? Do I have to paint a sign on my naked body and dance around the valley for you?" Shaking her head, she strode out of the cabin.

Her words had caught him completely off guard. Elise would have sulked, made him feel guilty. Abby had a temper that matched his, and worse, she had him imagining her dancing naked.

He shoved his hands in his pockets. He wondered what the sign said.

Two hours later, Holden was sitting atop his rig, ready to finish his journey to Crickhollow. He touched the rim of his floppy hat. "Abby, I appreciate the meal. Best I've had in a long time."

Abby smiled, pleased that her first guest had had a good time. "You're welcome any time."

The boys jumped up and down waving their goodbyes. Abby leaned down and whispered in each boy's ear a reminder and together they shouted "thank you."

Holden grinned. "Abby, I do believe you have found your place in the world."

Mr. Barrington stood behind her, his rigid stance as palpable as a touch. Her earlier annoyance hadn't completely faded and she was grateful that he had chores to do outside of the house for the next few hours.

"Be careful out there." Mr. Barrington's deep, rich voice made her skin tingle.

Holden's smile flattened to a grim line. "You be

careful, too. And keep a close eye on Miss Abby. When word spreads that there's a single woman here, the men will come sniffing around. Just a matter of time before some man snaps her up for his own.''

"Not on my watch." The cold steel in his voice sent a shiver down her spine. She had a glimpse of the man who'd been a bounty hunter.

Abby, Mr. Barrington and the boys all stood watching as Holden drove the coach down the rutted trail toward town. When his coach had vanished from sight, Abby was already thinking about what was to be done next. Holden's visit was a welcome change, but she had mending to do before laundry day tomorrow. "Quinn, Tommy, let's get you inside. You can practice your letters while I mend."

The boys scrambled toward the house and she was directly behind them when Matthias's strong hand settled on her shoulder.

She turned, shocked by his touch. They'd not touched once since their kiss last week. Foolish, she knew, but she had missed it. "Is something wrong?"

His stormy eyes met hers and she felt her stomach roll. "Do you know how to handle a gun?"

"A gun? No. My uncle kept a pistol in his desk." She'd seen it there once or twice. "There wasn't much call for guns in my section of San Francisco.''

The craggy lines in his face deepened. ''Then it's time you learned how to handle one.''

''For heaven's sakes, why?''

''The railroad is going to bring a lot of good to the valley and it'll bring trouble as well. I want you to know how to handle a gun.''

Her gaze dropped to the six-shooter in the well-worn holster hanging from his narrow hips. ''But you always carry a gun.''

''With all those horses to round up, I won't be around much. You'll need to know how to defend yourself.''

She brushed a stray wisp of hair from her face. ''I don't know the first thing about guns.''

''I do. Go fetch the boys from the cabin. I want to know exactly where they are when we start shooting targets. I'll get the shotgun from the barn.''

''Do you really think this is necessary?''

''Yes.''

''But I've got work.''

''It'll keep.''

Before she could say another word, he turned and headed toward the barn. Ten minutes later they stood beyond the corral, which now held Holden's tired team—two speckled geldings with black manes.

Matthias had hung six thick pieces of wood from a tree twenty paces away. Abby had settled the boys on a log behind them with orders for them not to move.

Abby's skirts and apron flapped in the breeze as she watched Matthias pull a shell from his vest pocket.

He flipped a small lever and cracked the gun in half and positioned a large shell at the opening. "You put the shell in this way. Make sure it's in good and tight, then close the gun." To illustrate, he snapped it closed with the ease of a man who'd done this a thousand times before.

She flinched. "That looks easy enough."

His gaze narrowed. "Now I want you to try it."

"I don't need to practice, do I? How hard can it be?"

He came up behind her and laid the gun in her hands. The smooth cold metal barrel and well-oiled wood stock felt heavy. Silent, he wrapped his arms around her and guided her hands to the right place on the stock.

His hard thighs pressed against her buttocks. She stood rigid, afraid to move forward or back.

He pointed to the small lever above the trigger

guard with a long, tanned finger. "This is the release switch. Flip it up and you can open the gun. Go ahead and open it. Show me how to take the slug out and put it back in."

Her heart beating against her ribs, she pushed the lever up.

"Good," he said, his face close to her ear. "Now, open the gun."

Gritting her teeth she pushed the barrel down. To her amazement, the gun opened easily. Inside the tip of the shell gleamed at her. With a bit of satisfaction, she pulled it out. "There."

"Excellent. Now put it back and close the gun."

She complied and was happy, if not a little relieved, to hand him back the gun.

"Now we shoot." He nodded toward the first branch. "Watch." He positioned the stock against his shoulder, lined up the first stick in his sights, then placed his finger on the trigger. He inhaled a deep breath, then exhaled slowly before he pulled the trigger.

The loud *crack* startled Abby as she watched the first stick explode in half. She glanced back at the boys who continued to play with their sticks.

"They've grown up around guns," he said, following her line of sight. "They're used to the sound."

She pressed her fingertip to her ear. "I didn't expect it to be so loud."

He motioned her forward. "Now it's your turn."

He reloaded the gun and stood beside her. "This gun's got one hell of a kick when you fire it, so I don't want you to hold it up to your shoulder when you shoot. Hold it next to your hip."

Matthias wrapped his arms around her and positioned the gun low against her hip. He moved the gun back and forth. "It'll jerk back when you fire it. Don't be afraid." He draped calloused fingers over her hand. "Now aim at what you want to hit, and then place your hand on the trigger and squeeze."

In the corner of her eye she saw the thick rich hair of his chest peeking out of the V formed by the unfastened buttons of his shirt. Her pulse quickened. Abby tore her gaze away and focused on the task at hand. Mimicking Mr. Barrington, she drew in a breath and let it out slowly. She pulled the trigger.

Ten paces ahead the dirt exploded in a plume of smoke.

"Looks like you managed to kill a patch of dirt," he said, a bit of humor in his voice.

Her hands trembling, she stared at the small uneven hole in the ground. "I was aiming at the tree over there."

His gaze trailed hers. "It takes practice. We'll work on it a little each day."

She arched an eyebrow. "A little each day? You mean until I leave?"

He stiffened. "Exactly."

That night when Matthias fell asleep, he dreamed of Abby.

In his dream, he climbed the ladder to her loft. She was waiting for him, lounging on a pillow, her long honey-blond hair loose over her naked breasts.

"I want you," she whispered.

His erection throbbed painfully as he slid off his pants and straddled her body. Candlelight glistened on her white skin. He slid his hand up her thigh over her flat belly. She felt hot and so very soft.

Her fingers skimmed over his shoulders and down his lean waist. She cupped his buttocks, lifting her pelvis, pressing her womanhood against his arousal.

Cupping the back of her head, he drew her up. Her nipples brushed his wiry chest hair, sending bolts of white-hot desire through him. He kissed her, pushing his tongue past her full lips. She moaned as her hand slid around and began to stroke him.

When he broke the kiss, he looked into her eyes. They flamed with a pure, sensuous hunger.

Neither spoke as he positioned himself at the center of her moist heat. In one swift move, he slid inside her. Her warm moisture enveloped him. He began to ride her, moving in and out as if he were half possessed. She moaned his name. He exploded inside her.

Matthias awoke with a start. His body was covered in a fine sheen of perspiration and he was breathing hard.

What was happening to him?

Chapter Ten

Over the next couple of days, the chilly days of spring quickly gave way to the hot, blistering ones of summer. Abby began to develop a routine with the boys and her chores, and she was starting to feel a measure of control.

Though Mr. Barrington worked his ranch during the day, he was home every day at sunset. He clearly hadn't forgotten Holden's warning.

The evenings quickly became Abby's favorite time. For a couple of brief hours the day's chores were done and with Mr. Barrington present, the cabin sizzled with an unspoken energy.

This evening, like the few before it, the four of them sat at the table by the lantern's glowing light. Mr. Barrington read to Tommy while she taught Quinn his letters. They were almost like a real family.

"M," Abby said. She and Quinn sat by the hearth. "M is for marmalade, mud and money."

"And Mom," Quinn said.

"That's right," Abby said.

Quinn looked up from the page and studied her. "Do you look like my mom?"

Mr. Barrington stopped, then laid down his book.

Abby kept her voice even. "I don't know, Quinn. I've never seen your ma."

"Pa," Quinn said turning immediately to his father. "Does Abby look like Ma?"

Lantern light glowed on his chiseled features. His gaze, a mixture of pain and frustration met hers. "No."

Abby set her piece of chalk down. She wanted for Mr. Barrington to expand on his answer. He didn't.

She glanced into Quinn's expectant eyes. "Maybe you could tell us what she looked like."

Quinn lifted his gaze to his father's. "Would you, Pa?"

Mr. Barrington's expression turned fierce as he looked over the boys' heads at Abby. His voice was barely a raspy whisper when he spoke. "You don't remember her?"

Quinn shook his head. "No, sir."

He sighed, his shoulders slumping a fraction.

"It's been over a year and you were only three at the time. I suppose it's natural." He closed the book gently. "She didn't look a thing like Abby. She was shorter and had blue eyes."

Abby was shocked to feel a pang of envy for Elise. The dead woman had borne two wonderful sons and had forever captured Mr. Barrington's heart. She hoped if she worked hard enough she could somehow make up for Elise's loss but as she looked into Quinn's young curious eyes, she knew he needed his memories of his mother. "Mr. Barrington, do you have a picture of Elise?"

His brows furrowed, he drew in a steadying breath before he glanced at the boys. They looked up at him with questioning expressions. "I do."

Abby sat a little straighter at the prospect of seeing the face of the woman whose memory had shadowed her since her arrival.

Mr. Barrington rose and walked to a chest that sat at the edge of his bed. Abby had dusted the chest with the initials EB carved on it a dozen times. She'd been sorely tempted to open it but hadn't.

Nervous anticipation sizzled in her veins as he lifted a worn Bible out. From the yellowed pages he pulled out two tintypes.

In the soft lantern light, Abby could see Mr. Barrington's face harden with sadness. Deliberately, he closed the chest and rose.

He sat back down at the table, his callous-tipped fingers closed over the tintype.

Abby's body itched with curiosity but she restrained herself. Folding her hands on her lap, she watched as the boys rose from their seats and stood beside their father.

Mr. Barrington unfurled his fingers and held the image close to the lamp. "This is your ma."

Quinn lay his small hand on Mr. Barrington's shoulder as he leaned closer. "How come she's not smiling?"

"Most people don't smile in pictures," Mr. Barrington said patiently. And then before the inevitable "why" came, he added, "You have to sit real still until a big flash goes off. It's easier not to smile."

"Why's she wearing a white dress?" Quinn said. "Didn't she worry about it getting dirty?"

Whereas Tommy preferred tree climbing and playing to his studies, his older brother was a thoughtful child, who lapped up every bit of learning tossed his way. He missed few details.

Mr. Barrington smiled. "It was her wedding dress. Actually, it had been her ma's dress. When women get married they often wear white."

''She's pretty,'' Quinn said.

''She was very beautiful,'' Mr. Barrington replied.

Feeling the interloper, Abby shoved aside her own interest and walked to the stove. She pulled a cup down from the shelf and poured a cup of lukewarm coffee for herself. Cradling the cup in her hands she listened as the boys asked questions about their mother.

''What's the other picture?'' Tommy asked.

Mr. Barrington set the first picture on the table. ''It's a picture of Quinn and your ma right after he was born.''

''Where am I?'' Tommy said.

Mr. Barrington smiled. ''You weren't born yet.''

''But I am now,'' he said.

''By the time you came along, we didn't have time to sit for pictures. There was so much going on. I promised your ma we'd have another family portrait done in the fall, but then she got sick.''

''She's pretty,'' Tommy said.

Abby sat back at the table. She set her cup down and as casually as she could manage, she picked up the first tintype. Her throat tightened as she looked into the beautiful face. Elise Barrington had smooth, clear skin and pale blue eyes. Ringlets the color of gold framed her oval face. The white silk dress trimmed with lace molded to her delicate shoulders and slender neck. Elise's pale eyes sparkled, as if she knew a secret no one else did. Abby had never learned to flirt. Joanne had been a master, but she'd found she was simply too straightforward to manage it.

As she looked at the picture, she felt clumsy and too tall. "She's lovely," she said.

When she looked up, she realized Mr. Barrington had been staring intently at her. In the lantern light his blue eyes looked sharper, more alert as if he were trying to read her mind.

Managing a faltering smile, she sipped her coffee. "May I see the other picture?"

Quinn handed it to her proudly. "That's me and my ma."

Elise sat in an upholstered chair and held a swaddled baby Quinn in her arms. Behind them stood Mr. Barrington, wearing a black suit, his hand on Elise's shoulder. Mr. Barrington looked proud and stared directly into the camera.

What struck Abby most about the picture was how much Elise had changed in the year and a half. Her eyes no longer possessed the coy spark. The ringlets had been traded for a tight chignon. Yet, despite the changes Elise was still a lovely woman.

"Quinn, you are a handsome baby," she said. "Why, you don't look bigger than a sack of sugar."

"He was a small baby," Mr. Barrington said. "But he had a cry that would shake the rafters."

Quinn looked closely at the picture. "I'm still pretty loud."

"You are indeed, son," Mr. Barrington said, laughing.

"Was I a small baby?" Tommy said.

Mr. Barrington ruffled his hair. "You were a big baby. Well over ten pounds. And you could cry just as loud as your brother."

Tommy looked at Quinn and grinned. He was clearly proud of his capacity to make noise.

Abby felt a twist in her heart. "I hope my babies are as handsome as you two boys."

Mr. Barrington's smile vanished instantly. He rose, lifting the boys under either arm. "It's time for bed, young bucks."

She knew she'd said something to make him angry. Already, she'd learned to gauge his moods.

He carried the boys to their large double bed. Earlier she'd washed their faces and hands and wiped their teeth with tooth powder. He tucked both under the covers, whispered something to them that made them smile, then kissed them good-night.

The nighttime ritual had fallen into a predictable

pattern. As soon as Mr. Barrington had finished his good-nights she moved in behind him. She and the boys said a simple prayer her mother had taught her and then she kissed the children.

Tonight though, the air was charged with energy. The pictures and her mention of children had left them both unsettled.

Mr. Barrington rose and walked outside to the front porch.

Abby followed him outside, quietly closing the door behind her. The air was crisp, but the sky was clear. Countless stars twinkled.

He turned around. Pale moonlight glowed on a fierce expression that took her breath away.

She leaned her shoulder against the rail post. "If that look is meant to frighten me, it doesn't. You might as well save it for the renegades and rustlers."

Respect flickered in his eyes before he turned. "I don't understand why you are here."

She struggled to keep the emotion out of her voice. "I like it."

"How could you like such a life? The work is backbreaking, the hours long."

"This place breathes life into me. I've never felt more alive in my life."

He tightened his hands over the railing. "Don't

set your heart on this place or me. You'll end up hurt or worse.''

She sighed impatiently. "You are a frustrating man, Mr. Barrington. I am in Montana because I want to be. I'm not chasing your dream, but my own."

"Then you're a fool."

She shrugged. "I've been called worse."

He studied her. "I don't understand you. Why come out here? Why didn't you marry in San Francisco? You are good wife material."

She laughed. "You make me sound like a plow or a chair."

Unrepentant, he shrugged. "It was meant as a compliment."

At first she wasn't sure if she'd answer him. San Francisco was far away now, and a part of her past forever. But Mr. Barrington had been nothing but honest with her and she owed him as much. "I was trapped between two worlds. My bloodlines put me above the servants yet I didn't have the social graces that elevated me to my aunt and uncle's station, either."

"So you carved out a place for yourself in the kitchens."

"It wasn't as bad as you make it sound. I was always so busy. My aunt and uncle had many parties and loved to show off my baking talents. Often I cooked for other families as a favor to my aunt and uncle. For a time I considered opening a bakery.''

''Why didn't you?''

''I wanted a family. I would have had little life outside of work if I owned a bakery.''

''And there was never anyone for you to love in a big city like San Francisco?'' She imagined a hint of jealousy underlined his words.

Crimson rose in her cheeks. ''There was, once.''

He leaned his head back against the porch post, studying her. ''What happened?''

She'd not spoken of Douglas to anyone in years. Her shame had run too deep. This conversation should have been awkward considering that they were strangers in so many ways. But talking to him was as natural as breathing. ''His name was Douglas. He was a distant relative of my aunt's visiting for the summer holiday. Immediately, he seemed to take a fancy to me. He was quite charming.''

Mr. Barrington grunted. ''I know the type.''

She shrugged. ''Unfortunately, I didn't. At the time I thought he was the best man in the world. He promised me the moon and I believed him.'' She leaned out over the railing and stared at the stars. They'd been the same stars she'd gazed at with Douglas so many years ago. The stars remained constant, while she was nothing like the girl who'd been fooled by a man who whispered words of love in her ear.

"He lied."

The night chill seeped into her bones. "Yes."

He was so close she could feel the heat of his body. He raised his hand and she thought for a moment he'd touch her. Instead, he let his hand drop. "You deserve a man who can give you a proper home and children, Abby."

"Yes, I realize that now."

A heavy silence rose between them. "I can never be that man."

"Why not?" The anguish in her voice was palpable.

"I'm used up. There's no love left in me."

Pride had her lifting her chin. "Ah, but that's where you make your mistake. Love is not what I am after. I simply want a place where I belong."

"Then you best leave here now. Because you don't belong here." He turned and strode toward the barn.

Her insides were quaking and for a moment she struggled with tears that welled in her eyes. A moment passed before she took a deep breath and regained control of herself.

Why was she doing this to herself? Why not take his advice and leave? She certainly didn't love the man.

Love.

She shook her head. No, not love. She'd never fall into that trap again.

Mr. Barrington had left a lantern glowing for her by the door. Picking it up, she returned inside the cabin, kissed each of the sleeping boys on their cheeks then climbed the small ladder up to her loft. Too restless to sleep, she knelt on her pallet. The lantern burned softly as she changed out of her work dress into a nightgown and unpinned her hair. Unbound, it teased the top of her hips.

She picked up her brush from beside her pallet along with a silver mirror that had belonged to her mother. She started to brush her hair, counting out her nightly one hundred strokes.

Abby knew she was a hard worker. She was dependable. Mr. Barrington had already come to rely on her. She'd taken over the morning and evening milking of the cows and he trusted her completely with the boys.

But did he find her attractive?

Her mind drifted to that first picture of Elise. The young girl had exuded feminine charm. It had been her eyes and the slight quirk of her lips.

Abby picked up the silver-backed mirror and glanced at her reflection.

The sprinkle of freckles across the bridge of her nose had always made her look younger, less sophisticated. And she'd never been fond of her nose, far too short and perky.

Abby glanced down her nightgown. Her breasts were large and full, and it had been her experience that men liked large breasts. More than once she'd caught the butler looking at her body. But she wasn't petite like Elise.

She propped her mirror against the wall and held her hair up in a looser, more fashionable hairstyle.

The style didn't suit. No amount of fancy hairstyles or perfume would ever make her as pretty as Elise.

She touched her fingertips to her lips, remembering Mr. Barrington's kiss. In that moment they had seemed to fit together very well, almost as if their bodies had been fashioned with the other in mind.

Frustrated, Abby laid her head against her pillow, then rolled on her side and blew out the lantern. She lay in the dark staring into the utter blackness. Slowly sleep crept through her limbs.

Abby had nearly drifted completely off when she heard the howl of wolves. At first she thought it a dream and rolled on her side away from the door, hugging the blanket close to her chin.

But then she heard Mr. Barrington get out of bed. She'd not imagined the sounds. He'd heard them, too.

She sat up to the sound of him pulling on his pants and boots. Leather rubbed against the bed-post—he'd reached for his gun belt, which always stayed within arm's reach.

Her fatigue vanished and in an instant her heart hammered against her chest. Where was he going? In the weeks she'd been here, she'd never known him to stir at night.

Steady purposeful steps echoed in the cabin as he moved to the front door. The door opened, then closed.

Abby strained to hear. There was the sound of the boys' deep even breathing. The distant howl of a coyote.

An unsettled feeling seeped into the marrow of her bones.

Something was wrong.

In the dark, Abby felt around for her boots then slipped them on. Next, she searched for her shawl. When she found it at the base of her pallet, she tossed it over her shoulders.

If she had any sense, she'd have lit a lantern. But

Mr. Barrington had not. What she'd heard outside had not been a dream. He'd heard it, too.

Gingerly, she eased down the ladder. She'd spent enough time in this cabin to know its furnishings and layout by heart. To her left was the kitchen and to her right the bed where the boys slept.

Despite her familiarity with the room the night's utter blackness threw off her senses and she found herself moving more slowly than normal.

She bumped hard into the front door, stubbing her toe.

Pain shot up her leg and tears flooded her eyes. "Blast," she whispered. Gripping her toe she drew in deep, even breaths until the pain passed.

She eased her weight back down onto her injured toe, testing it, until she was certain she'd not broken it.

Slowly, she lifted the latch and cracked open the front door. Easing outside, she closed the door quietly behind her.

Abby took one step when strong arms clamped over her mouth and banded around her waist. She was dragged against a hard-muscled chest.

Chapter Eleven

Abby should have been afraid, but she wasn't.

She was mad that someone would come onto *her* porch and accost her after all the sweat and time she'd invested. With Mr. Barrington nowhere in sight, she wondered if this cretin had ambushed Mr. Barrington, as well.

Fear sliced through her as she pictured him bleeding and injured. Desperate to find him, she did the first thing that came to mind. She drove the heel of her boot into her attacker's shin.

Save for a soft grunt, her attacker made no sound. Instead, he tightened his hold, and, lifting her off her feet, carried her toward the barn.

Abby struggled, her shawl dropped to the porch, but her efforts accomplished nothing, other than draining her own strength. She tried to kick her assailant again but each time he was ready for her, sidestepping her attacks easily.

"Stop fighting me, damn it!"

At the sound of Mr. Barrington's gruff voice, Abby froze. He half drug, half carried her across the yard to the barn. Kicking the barn door open with his foot, he pulled her inside and then closed it. He flipped her around and pressed her back against the door. She stared up into his shadowed face, just inches from hers. His hot breath brushed her cheek.

"Why did you grab me?" she whispered.

"There's someone or something outside."

She moistened her lips, which still tasted salty from his hand. With only her nightgown, she was very aware of her nakedness. "Who?"

"I was trying to find out when you came outside."

She ignored the irritation in his voice. "I heard you get up and leave. I thought there was a problem."

"There is. Now stay put."

"Don't you need a light?"

"No." He eased his gun from its holster and started to move outside, his actions as graceful and lethal as a mountain lion.

Abby started to follow.

Mr. Barrington stopped. "Stay put."

"I can help."

"Stay." His order sliced through the night air, cutting through any future arguments. When he was certain she'd obey, he disappeared into the night.

In the distance, the howl of wolves echoed in the dark. Abby's heart slammed against her rib cage.

The boys! Abby remembered the boys were in the cabin alone. What if whoever or whatever was out there doubled back and took the boys? Unable to stay in the barn, Abby fumbled around until her fingers skimmed the handle of a pitchfork. Holding it high, she peeked out of the barn.

At first she didn't see Mr. Barrington. Then she saw the glitter of moonlight on the barrel of his gun. He moved across the yard, a wraith moving as if he'd been born to roam the night.

Abby's fingers bit into the handle of the pitchfork. Drawing in a deep breath, she watched him move into the shadows and out of sight.

Immediately, she ran across the yard toward the house, her flimsy gown billowing in the night. Quickly, she looked in on the boys. Certain they were fine, she closed the front door and stood guard.

Tense minutes passed. Finally, Mr. Barrington

strode out of the dark toward the porch. He'd already figured out she wasn't in the barn.

He holstered his gun as he approached. "*Stay put.* What part of those words don't you understand?"

The bunched muscles in her back relaxed at the sound of his voice. "I was protecting the boys."

He glanced at the pitchfork. "Next time, get the gun."

She'd forgotten all about the gun. She felt foolish. "It was too dark."

"Lesson number one. Never come outside at night without it. Keep it under your pillow if you must. If it's not a stranger it could just as easily be a bear."

A bear. She'd seen a bear in the circus once. It looked soft and furry. "Was it a bear?"

"I think so." The dark made his features unreadable, but anger singed his words.

"Do they come this close often?"

He glanced toward the moonlit horizon, his face hard. "Often enough."

"I saw a bear in a carnival once. It looked friendly enough. It wore a red vest and a laced collar."

He looked at her as if she'd gone daft. "They

can tear you to shreds with one swipe of their claws.''

"Oh.''

He tapped his finger against his gun handle. He reached past her for the lantern that hung by the front door. Pulling a match from his pocket he lit it.

"Maybe it won't come back.''

"It will.''

"How can you be sure?''

"When an animal comes this close to a homestead, it's grown bold. I start corralling the horses tomorrow, and I don't like the idea of a bear this close to the homestead.'' Buttery, warm light had Abby squinting until her eyes adjusted. Mr. Barrington held up the lantern and studied the ground.

"You're not going after it tonight, are you?'' she asked.

"No, it's too dark, but I wanted to see if there were any tracks in the yard.'' He turned and moved off the porch toward the barn and stopped.

Abby followed him. "What are we looking for?''

He knelt and pressed his fingertips into a large indentation of a claw in the dirt. "Tracks.''

Her hair fell forward as she held up her lantern and leaned forward to study the dirt. "How can you tell much? I mean, it could be another animal.''

He gently touched the imprint burrowed in the dirt. "It's a bear. A male, judging by the size of the foot."

"Oh."

"He favors a paw. If he's injured he'll be more dangerous."

"Good Lord, you can tell that by just one track?"

"Yes."

"Can you tell what color it is?" she asked flippantly.

He glared up at her.

She shrugged and pretended to stare harder at the dirt. "It looks like just dirt to me."

He shoved his fingers through his hair. "I won't be able to get a true read on these tracks until morning. Then I can follow it and find out where it came from."

"Who taught you all this?"

He rose, his gaze aimed toward the distant horizon. "An Indian tracker for the army."

Yet another facet to a man she knew so little about. "You've certainly had a checkered career." Nervous laughter bubbled inside her. "To be honest it's all I can do to follow street signs with a map."

A half smile curved his lips as he turned.

However, all traces of humor vanished when he

faced her. The glow of the lantern accented the hard planes of his face. His shirt was open and the thick mat of hair curled on his broad chest. His eyes darkened with an earthy intensity that had her flesh puckering into gooseflesh. The air between them sizzled.

Her nipples hardened and her breathing grew shallow. "Is something the matter?" she said, her voice little more than a hoarse whisper.

Silent, his gaze moved leisurely and boldly up her body. "Your lantern."

Self-conscious, she raised her lantern. "What about my lantern?"

"Its light makes your gown transparent."

Matthias could not lift his gaze from the near-naked swell of Abby's breasts. His mouth watered as he stared at the threadbare nightgown that molded to her full, taut breasts and nipples.

He flexed his fingers, praying for the strength to walk away. None came.

Slowly, he lifted his gaze to hers, half hoping to see shock or outrage in her green eyes. Anything to jolt him out of this raw lust pulsing in his veins.

What he found was desire, albeit hesitant and untried, in her green eyes. She moistened her lips.

Dear Lord, she truly looked as if she wanted him as much as he wanted her.

His erection throbbed. Sanity vanished.

Matthias took the lantern from Abby and blew it out. Then in one swift move, he wrapped his arms around her narrow waist. She came willingly, encircling her arms around his neck. Her breasts strained against the fabric and pressed against his chest.

Her long hair, a rich waterfall of curls, teased the top of her waist as she tipped her head back. Her lips parted.

Matthias kissed Abby on the mouth. Her lips opened and his tongue slid into the warm, wet depth of her mouth. A soft moan rumbled in her chest, and she rubbed her flat belly against him.

He tightened his grip, threading his fingers into the silken mass of her hair. Her desire fanned his and before he thought too much, he backed her up several paces and had pressed her against the side of the barn. His legs braced apart, her thigh pressed seductively over his hardness.

Abby tipped back her head and he kissed the soft hollow of her neck. Her pulse hammered under her tender skin. Her blood raced like his.

Matthias's hand slid down her firm thigh. He grabbed a handful of her nightgown and yanked it up until his hand touched bare skin. He squeezed her naked buttocks. She arched, her fingers biting into his back.

He kissed the center of her collarbone, then moved south to the top of her right breast. Hindered by the fabric, he sucked her nipple through the nightgown until it hardened into a peak.

Breathless, he lifted his gaze to hers. Her eyes were half open and her gaze shrouded by the dewy haze of passion. Months of pent-up desire exploded. Consequences be damned. He'd have her now.

"Inside the barn," he said, his voice as rough as the jagged rock of the distant mountain peaks.

She moistened her lips again, nodding. "Yes."

He gave her buttocks one last squeeze then shoved open the barn door. "There's a fresh bale of hay in the corner."

She followed him to the sweet earthy hay and lay down on her back. Leaning back on her elbows, she stared up at him. Her gown was hiked up past her knees. The top four buttons were unfastened, creating a low V between her breasts. The creamy mounds created a seductive cleavage.

Matthias fell to the straw. Grabbing her behind the knees, he yanked her to him before he positioned his body between her legs. Cupping her right breast with one hand he cradled her neck with the other. He kissed her again, devouring the taste of her. Her hands eased under his shirt up his back.

Matthias lost track of time. He didn't know how long he kissed her, fondled her, but by the time he rose and reached for his belt buckle, his blood boiled with desire.

He unfastened the buckle and then the top three buttons. He ached for release.

Abby lowered her gaze to his pants, staring expectantly. She'd never seen a fully naked man before but in truth nothing felt more right or natural. Soon, she would understand what the women in the kitchens talked brazenly about, what they all craved so much, what Douglas had just begun to inspire in her.

The throbbing in her body was like nothing she'd ever known. She could feel her own dampness and though she didn't understand it, knew it was right. With only nature and meager experience as her guide, she slid her hand down his flat belly. He hissed in a breath. He wanted her. And she marveled at the power of her womanhood.

Matthias reached inside his pants and pulled *it* out. For a moment she could only stare in shock and wonder. Though she understood the logic of what was about to happen, in truth she couldn't imagine how *it* was going to fit.

Matthias pushed up her nightgown. He draped his body over hers, only this time the tip of his manhood pressed against her soft, moist opening.

Deep in her heart, she understood that once they joined, they would in some way be bonded forever. There would be no going back for Abby.

This moment was nothing like she'd ever imagined, and yet it was better. There were no soft words or poetry, only a raw need. But she needed something from him. She wasn't naive enough to expect words of love, but she needed to know it was *her* he was making love to.

She stroked the hard muscles of his buttocks. "Say my name," she whispered, her voice so husky she barely recognized it.

The lust in his veins had stolen his voice, his ability to speak in clear sentences. He pressed his arousal against her opening, poised to thrust.

She wriggled, so that he fell away from her opening. "Say my name."

The corded muscles in his neck strained as he repositioned himself. Sweat dampened his brow. Closing his eyes, he began to push inside her.

Her body wanted to feel him inside her. Her heart needed to her him say her name.

He pushed inside her. She felt the searing pain as her maidenhood tore, and all reasonable thoughts vanished. Her entire body tensed. He paused, realizing what he'd taken from her.

He began to move inside of her, his movements slow at first but quickly building to a fever pitch.

Raw need pulsed inside her.

Dear Lord, what was he doing to her? Sweat formed between her breasts.

"Wrap your legs around me," he whispered.

She complied, taking him inside her fully. Her body stretched and molded around him. She didn't think she could feel more alive. Then he reached for her moist center and began to stroke.

She hissed in a breath. "What are you doing to me?"

"Shh, it's all right." He continued to stroke, circling her softness with expert precision. The fever inside of her grew. Her senses reeled. She teetered at the cliff of an unknown abyss.

And then, in a flash, her body exploded in sensations. She moaned and arched her back, letting the ripples wash over her body.

Mr. Barrington withdrew his hand and began to pump harder. And in the next instant, his body tensed and as he found his release, he moaned. "Elise."

* * *

Matthias knew his blunder the instant he'd whispered Elise's name. A bucket of cold water couldn't have made Abby's languid body tense faster. She went rigid.

She pressed her palms against his chest. "Get off me."

Her voice seemed to come from a very far-off place though her lips were just by his ears.

But as he felt her struggles underneath him grow in strength he forced himself to roll off her.

Immediately, she scrambled out from under him and tugged her nightgown over her legs, now tucked under her. "You called me Elise."

Lying on his back, he stared up at the barn's rafters. "It was an accident."

Tears burned her eyes. "Some accident."

He stabbed his hands through his hair. "It's been six years since there's been another woman."

Her long hair cascaded over her shoulder draping breasts he'd just suckled. "You don't want me. You wanted to use my body."

Though Abby's body felt nothing like Elise's, he couldn't deny her words. A part of him had wanted to resurrect his old love. He tugged up his pants and fastened the four buttons. "I'm sorry."

Unshed tears glistened in her eyes. "I thought

for just a few moments it was just you and me. I was wrong.''

He shoved impatient fingers through his thick hair. ''I'm sorry.''

Slowly, she rose. Moonlight cascaded on her gown. That's when he noticed the streaks of blood. Earlier, he'd felt her tightness, but his befuddled mind hadn't fully processed the consequences. Now the full weight of his mistake sank in.

She lifted her head high, like a proud warrior goddess. ''You win. You were right. I don't belong here.''

Abby started to move past him. He sprang to his feet and grabbed her arm. She looked up with eyes filled with sorrow and shame.

''It's not that simple anymore,'' he said. Even now, touching her sent desire ricocheting through him.

She jerked her arm free of his hold. ''It is for me, *Mr. Barrington.*''

''I think you should call me Matthias now.''

''I'd rather not.'' Her prickly tone reminded him of the first time he'd seen her in the stage—Society Miss.

He stared at the trail of blood on her gown. ''I'm sorry.''

She followed his gaze. Her cheeks flamed red,

and she covered the fresh spots of blood with her hand.

"I thought you'd been with another man," he said, his voice hoarse. "You said your reputation was ruined."

"One does not have to be guilty to be convicted."

He rubbed the back of his neck, now tight with tension. "I'm sorry."

She tipped back her head as a tear streamed down her cheek. "Stop saying that." She started toward the door.

He grabbed her wrist. "Like it or not, we are bound together now."

"Nothing binds us except business. I'll stay to the end of the summer or until you can arrange to find someone to take care of the boys."

He ground his teeth. She wasn't going anywhere. "You could be pregnant."

Shock widened her eyes. Her hands flew to her flat belly. For an instant joy flashed in her eyes. "That's not possible. It was only one time."

"Once is sufficient," he said more tersely than he'd intended. "Take my word for it, there could be a baby."

She shook her head. "There isn't. I'd know if there was."

"How the hell would you know? Do you have the second sight?"

She lifted her chin, again the proud city woman. "I just would *know*." Wouldn't she?

Annoyed, he ground his teeth. "Well, I'm glad you're so all-knowing but you'll have to excuse me for being a little slower."

The menace in his voice triggered alarm bells in her. "What are you talking about?"

"Until I know for certain you aren't pregnant, you're not going anywhere."

"I can take care of myself. And *my* baby if need be."

His temper held on by a thread. He needed time to think and more time to fix this mess he'd created. "No other man is ever going to raise *my* child. I take care of my own. You're not leaving this ranch until I know for certain that you're not carrying a child."

"You said you didn't want any more children!"

"I don't. But I'll stand by any I make."

Her eyes looked wild, desperate. And it tore at him that he'd robbed the sparkle from her eyes.

"You can't keep me here," she said.

His resolve, like forged iron, was unbreakable. "Watch me."

Chapter Twelve

*H*e'd called her Elise!

Still hurt two days later, she stared out the kitchen window watching the boys who were poking a stick in a rabbit hole. She enjoyed the boys and had been growing to love them as her own. But since that night in the barn she'd realized she had been fooling herself. They weren't her children and never would be. They belonged to Elise. Just as everything else in this blasted cabin belonged to her.

Abby sighed as she ran a soapy washcloth over a tin plate. She had only herself to blame for this mess. Mr. Barrington had been clear about his feelings from the start. He had said he had loved his first wife with all his heart. He had said he didn't have room in his heart for love. But she'd thought if she worked hard enough, hoped hard enough, she could make everything come together. She thought she could change him. How wrong she'd been.

She'd been such a fool.

Tears glistened in her eyes and she tilted her head back so that they wouldn't spill.

She and Mr. Barrington had barely spoken since that night. He'd left at first light the next morning, determined to track the bear and begin rounding up the horses. He'd told her it could take a day or two before he returned. Reminding her to keep the rifle close, he'd left.

She rinsed the dish and laid it on a drying towel by the sink.

The one ray of hope to rise from this disaster was the possibility of a baby. She imagined cradling the child close, savoring the soft scents of milk. Her baby. She tried to imagine what their child would look like. Likely black hair like Mr. Barrington and the boys. Fair skin.

Someone to love *her*.

Abby gave herself a mental shake. A baby would also complicate things far too much. A baby would bind her to a man who could never love her. She'd not come looking for love but she realized how much she wanted it now.

She quickly finished the dishes and turned her

attention to the rising bowls of dough on the counter. She had two loaves cooling, two baking and three more to set up. Holden's first coach full of passengers was due sometime today, and she wanted to be ready for him. A thick stew simmered on the stove, and she'd made cheese and butter yesterday.

Abby thought about the hard cash she'd earn today. How much would she make and how long would it be before she could buy a train ticket out of Montana?

"Abby," Quinn shouted from the door. "The stage is coming."

Abby glanced out the window. Realizing she still had a few minutes, she quickly shaped the rising dough into loaves and laid them on the rising board. She covered the dough with a tea cloth and wiped her hands on her apron.

She gave the cabin a quick glance to make certain everything was in place. She'd pressed and ironed her grandmother's tablecloth and set it with the mismatched selection of flatware that Mr. Barrington owned. A chipped mug filled with wildflowers adorned the center of the table.

A paltry presentation by her aunt and uncle's standards, but in the wilds of Montana a hot meal and fine linen tablecloth were nothing short of a

miracle. The coach riders would be *her* first customers. And she wanted everything to be perfect.

Satisfied, she went outside.

The sun was bright and hot and the sky crystal-
clear. The boys jumped up and down by her skirts
clapping their hands.

"You two settle down now," she said. "We've
got guests to take care of."

"Candy!" Tommy shouted.

Abby knelt down. "Now don't be asking Holden
about candy. It's polite to wait. And remember to
say please and thank you."

"Okay," Quinn said.

Tommy squirmed, too excited to stand still.

She wiped a smudge of dirt from his nose and,
smiling, stood. "Now run out and play."

Skimming her hands on her skirt, she watched as
the coach rumbled down the dusty trail. Puffs of
dirt swirled around the coach wheels as the horses'
hooves dug into the earth. In the driver's seat sat
Holden, his dark hat pulled low over his eyes.

Holden pulled the wagon to a stop fifty feet from
the front door. Before he could tie off the reins the
door to the coach opened. A tall lanky man dressed
in gray stepped out of the coach. He wore a floppy
hat and carried a knapsack on his shoulder.

Another man emerged from the coach. Short with

a muscular build, he wore denim workpants and a faded red shirt.

Holden hopped down from the driver's seat. He smiled at Abby, touching the brim of his hat. "Good to see you again, Miss Abby."

Abby felt her sprits lift. It was nice to have company. "You're looking fit, Holden."

He sauntered toward her. "Can't complain. Like for you to meet your first customers. This is Mr. Webber," he said pointing to the tall man. "And this is Mr. Pike. They're headed up north to survey lines for the railroad. Both have come a long way and are hungry as bears."

She nodded to both men. "It's a pleasure. I've a pot full of stew, bread baking in the oven and more rising."

"Ma'am," Mr. Webber said. "Your words couldn't be sweeter if you were an angel."

Mr. Pike pressed his hand against his belly. "I could eat a bear. And if I may say ma'am, you're a sight for sore eyes. Haven't seen a woman in two months."

Self-conscious, she smoothed a loose strand of hair back down. "Thank you."

"Obliged," Mr. Pike said.

"Where do you gentleman call home?" Abby asked.

Mr. Pike pulled off his hat. ''I'm from Ohio and Mr. Webber is all the way from Maryland.''

''So you gentlemen are setting the course for this new railroad I've been hearing so much about?'' She'd heard a few tales from Mrs. Clements of the men who worked the advance party of the rail lines. All a breed apart, these men made their own rules.

Mr. Webber took his hat off. ''Yes ma'am. Railroad is paying top dollar, and I'm hoping to make enough money to buy me a farm back home.''

Mr. Pike hooked his thumbs in his belt. ''Takes a lot of money to outweigh the risks. But so far, it's been worth it.''

Dreams. She'd come to this land with dreams. ''Well, I wish you both the best of luck. There's a barrel of fresh rainwater on the side of the house if you want to wash your hands and face. The water's cold but clean. Now wash up and I'll have your supper ready in fifteen minutes.''

As she turned toward the cabin, she caught sight of a rider galloping toward the house. A glance at the black mare told her it was Mr. Barrington. He sat tall in his saddle, his muscular thighs hugging the horse with ease. A familiar black Stetson shadowed his eyes.

Even at this distance, the sight of him made her stomach flutter. She could feel the familiar weakness in her limbs. She closed her eyes, her mind immediately turning to the night in the barn.

Instead of waiting for him as she might have done a week ago, she lifted her skirt and went inside the house. Her eyes adjusting to the dimmer light, she noted her hands trembled a little as she started to pull down the plates and set the table for her guests.

Mr. Barrington's deep masculine voice echoed across the front lawn and into the house. Her spine pricked with unwelcome sensations and she cursed her body for not having the sense to ignore him as her mind was so desperately trying to do.

Minutes passed as she sliced bread and ladled hot stew into the bowls. She filled cups with fresh milk then checked the chokeberry pie she had cooling on the sill.

The boards on the steps creaked, signaling the arrival of her guests. Smoothing a stray lock of hair from her forehead, she turned and smiled. "Well, come right in."

Instantly, her smile vanished. In the doorway stood Mr. Barrington, his broad shoulders all but blocking out the noonday sun. Dark stubble covered his chin and his long hair was tied at the base of his neck with a strip of rawhide. He looked more like a desperado than a rancher.

His hat in hand he stepped inside the cabin. His spurs jingled as he walked toward her.

"Where are Holden and the others?" She readjusted the forks on the napkins for the tenth time today.

"Using the outhouse, stretching their legs. Holden is unsaddling my horse. They'll be here in a minute."

Even after two days, having him this close made her stomach flutter. "Did you have luck finding the bear?" she said coolly.

"No, I lost his tracks about half a mile from here." He hung up his hat on a peg by the door. "I thought by now you'd be calling me Matthias."

She took an extra moment to smooth out the last napkin, needing some simple task to keep her nerves steady. "That seems a little familiar."

He lifted an eyebrow. "Too familiar? After what happened?"

"I'd rather keep things more formal."

"It's too late for that."

Her hands started to shake. "Are you hungry?"

His dark gaze locked on her in a too-familiar way. "Yes."

She could feel the color rising in her cheeks but she turned toward the cupboard before he could see.

"Let me set you a place then. You can visit with our guests."

A heavy silence settled in the room as she set another plate, fork and cup on the table.

His gaze bore into her. "It's rare we have time in the middle of the day to talk."

Color burned her cheeks. "We don't have time. Our guests will be here any moment."

"I asked Holden to see that we had a couple of minutes."

Her head snapped up. Her throat felt as dry as dust. "Why?"

He leaned against the counter. His stance seemed casual, but his gaze was harder than steel. "Like it or not we need to talk."

The wind howled against the cabin, making it creak. "If you're wondering about the baby, I don't know anything yet."

"When will you know?" he said stiffly.

Tears glistened in her eyes. "A week, maybe sooner."

He shifted, uncomfortable as if talking was the last thing he wanted to do. "Look, Abby, there's more to talk about other than the baby."

"I don't think so, Mr. Barrington. I'll be leaving at the end of the summer as we discussed." A tear escaped and she savagely wiped it away. "Now if you'll excuse me. I've got to finish getting the table ready.''

Annoyance flashed in his eyes but he went silent. He glanced down at the table. There were three places plus the one she'd added for him. ''Aren't you joining us?''

''No, I thought I'd take the boys outside and keep them out of everyone's way. It can be hard to eat a meal when they're running about.''

''I want you to sit, relax for a few minutes.''

''I've never been one for sitting and relaxing.''

Before either could speak another word the men filed inside the cabin. With so many people in the single room, the space felt painfully small. Mr. Barrington was only inches from her, and the heat from his body scalded her skin.

Abby wished the cabin had more space. Her mind drifted toward a project she'd considered from the start—adding on another room. Perhaps expand the kitchen, and then she could bake extra goods and send them into town with Holden for Mrs. Clements to sell in her store.

She caught herself.

She was leaving soon.

There wouldn't be any need for the expansion because, once she left, Holden would stop bringing customers by for a meal.

Sadness tugged at her before she refocused on the men who stared at the food with longing.

"Dig in, gentlemen," Abby said. "Don't wait on my account. Enjoy your lunch."

Needing no other encouragement, the men grabbed slices of bread from the platter in the middle of the table. They started to eat.

Mr. Barrington stood with his back straight. He looked ready to turn on his heel and leave when Holden arrived. "I turned the horses loose in the corral and I washed my hands." There was a wide grin on Holden's face as he held up his hands to Abby. "Quinn told me you're a stickler for clean hands."

She grinned. Having him in the cabin diffused the tension and she felt as if she could breathe again. "Have a seat. I'd say you pass inspection."

Holden glanced up at Mr. Barrington. "Aren't you going to have a seat? Shame to waste a hot meal."

A muscle pulsed on the side of his jaw. "I'll sit if Abby does."

She took a step back. "I thought I'd leave you men to your meal. And I really should check on the boys."

"The boys are playing inside the coach," Holden

said quickly. "I told them no climbing on top." He popped a piece of bread in his mouth. "Sit."

Mr. Barrington pulled a spare chair from the corner and placed it directly beside his. "Don't want to disappoint our guests, Abby."

She ground her teeth. He was backing her into a corner and they both knew she was too damn polite to make a scene in front of company.

With no other choice, she took the seat he held for her. Only when she was seated did he take his. The space was cramped. She scooted her chair an inch from his only to have him move his two inches toward her. The casual brush sent fire through her veins and for a moment she thought she'd jump out of her skin.

Mr. Barrington, however, looked perfectly content where he was. He snapped open his napkin and laid it across his lap. "Pike and Webber, is it?"

"Yes, sir," Mr. Pike said. "And I got to say that this is the best food I've eaten since I left home."

"Brings tears to my eyes, ma'am," Mr. Webber said.

Abby barely heard what they said. "Thank you."

The men started talking about the work they'd been doing and the harsh weather they'd seen since they'd arrived. Abby let the conversations drift over her head.

Guests were so rare and she wanted to sit and chat, but having Mr. Barrington so close was making her nerves dance. His scent enveloped her. Her stomach tightened each time he shifted in his seat and brushed her thigh.

She needed distance and space.

Abby glanced toward the door hoping the boys needed her so that she could escape Mr. Barrington's presence. She saw Quinn's head pop out of the stagecoach window and then Tommy's out of the other. Both were laughing.

"I better go check on the children," she said.

"The boys are fine," Mr. Barrington said smoothly. He laid his hand on her knee. "Enjoy this time."

Enjoy. His touch scorched through her skirt to her flesh. She felt ready to jump out of her skin.

"How long have you two been out here, Mr. Barrington?" Mr. Pike asked. He dunked his bread into his stew and popped it in his mouth.

"I've had the homestead for almost five years," Mr. Barrington said. He deliberately withheld the fact that she'd only just arrived.

Abby fluffed her napkin. "I've only been here two weeks."

The miners seemed surprised by her answer and

she could feel Mr. Barrington's scowl bearing down on her.

"So how do you like Montana, ma'am?" Mr. Webber said.

"It's lovely country."

"A backbreaker if you ask me," Mr. Pike said.

"Still," Webber added, "it's tolerable if a man has his wife with him."

Abby pinched a piece of bread. "Oh, Mr. Barrington and I aren't married. I only work for him."

Matthias thought Pike and Webber were going to jump out of their seats. A woman in these parts was rare. But a single one as lovely as Abby was a miracle.

The men sat straighter. Mr. Webber sucked in his stomach. Their horns were up and they were already thinking about how they'd snag Abby for their own.

Over his dead body.

The raw possessiveness surprised Matthias but he didn't question it. Though he'd blundered things badly between them, these railroad men weren't going to complicate matters more. He knew how these surveyors lived. They worked from sun-up to sun-down and slept in hovels at night. The thought of

Abby carving out an existence on the line grated his nerves.

"Miss Abby," Mr. Pike said. "You ever traveled up to the northern part of the territory?"

She smiled, completely unaware that the man was likely undressing her with his eyes as they spoke. "I've not had the pleasure."

"I been thinking about going up there to try my hand in the gold fields. I hear miners are finding gold faster than they can shove it in their pockets," he said. "Why, this time next month, I'm liable to be a millionaire."

Matthias grit his teeth. Flat broke was more like it.

"Ma'am, if I may be so bold, you are about the prettiest woman I ever did see," Mr. Webber said.

Abby glanced up and blushed prettily.

Dear Lord, she wasn't falling for that bounder's line. "So are you gentlemen headed out after lunch?" he said to Holden.

Holden glanced up from his stew. "I thought we'd stay a spell. Rest our bones."

Mr. Webber, his belly full, was leering. Horny bastard.

"The weather looks like it could close in," Matthias warned. His words were casual, while his meaning was predatory. Get off my land! "You best head out right after lunch so you don't get caught in a storm.''

Holden frowned. ''The sky is clear as a bell.''

Abby paused, her cup near her lips. ''Holden's right, there's not a cloud in the sky.''

''It's going to rain,'' Matthias growled.

Holden glanced up. When he saw Matthias's murderous expression, he glanced toward the men who gawked at Abby. He understood in an instant. ''I suppose it would be best if we made Crickhollow by dark.''

''The sooner the better.''

Abby frowned. ''Are you sure? We don't get guests very often.''

Holden ate faster, as if sensing Matthias's patience was now paper-thin. ''Don't worry, I'll be back.''

Thirty minutes later, Matthias, Abby and the children waved goodbye as Holden pulled out with his passengers.

Once the stage had left, Abby started back toward the cabin, with the boys in tow.

''Abby, I'd like to speak to you.'' Matthias watched her turn, noted the worry and concern on her face. ''Boys, run on inside while I talk to Miss Abby.''

The boys scurried into the cabin, leaving Abby

alone to face him. "I have to clean up the lunch plates."

"They'll keep." He had hoped two days on the trail would cool his desire for her and give his mind time to clear. It hadn't worked.

Each night, his mind filled with thoughts of how well their bodies fit together. Even now he remembered the soft warmth of her skin.

When he'd been with Elise, he'd always kept a tight rein on his needs, fearing if she saw the animal need in him, she would be afraid. With Abby, he'd lost control. His animal desires had roared to life. But there'd been no fear in Abby's eyes. Instead there'd been a fire in her that had matched his own. Under all that calico beat the heart of a passionate woman.

Pent-up desires pulled at the bit.

The intent in his eyes had her backing away a step. "What can I do for you, Mr. Barrington?"

Shoving his hands in his pockets, Matthias straightened his shoulders. He wasn't sure how he was going to mend things with Abby, but he had to fix the mess he'd created. "Those men here today. You understand what they're after."

She lifted an eyebrow. "I have a fair idea."

"Don't be fooled by their words."

"I won't be fooled again."

He caught her meaning. Seeing those other men ogling her drove home the fact that he could easily lose her. He was painfully aware now what he was losing. What he'd had with Abby.

"There'll be others like them."

"Only if I'm lucky." She grinned wickedly, turned on her heel and flounced into the house.

"You won't be entertaining men on my land, under my roof."

She shrugged. "I came out here for a fresh start. That's what I plan to have. If a man comes calling, I won't chase him off."

Possessive hot need pounded in his veins. If he had his way, he'd toss her over his shoulder, take her in the barn and make love to her right now. "Then I will," he growled.

Challenge snapped in Abby's eyes. "So let me understand this. *You* can't move on with your life and you won't let me move on with *mine*."

No. Yes. "Damn it. You're making it sound more complicated than it is."

"I think it's best for all of us if I leave on the next stage. Mrs. Clements will watch the boys if I ask her and then you can be free to do your work and mourn your dead wife." Her cheeks flushed. "Consider this my notice, Mr. Barrington."

Before he could respond, she turned on her heel and marched back into the cabin.

Matthias stood with his hands clenched at his sides.

Abby wasn't going anywhere.

She was his.

Chapter Thirteen

Later that afternoon, Abby sat on a log under the shade of a poplar tree churning butter. Her anger had cooled and she now regretted losing her temper. What was wrong with her? Her emotions were all over the place.

Emotions had turned her life into a disastrous mess eight years ago and now they were doing it again. She'd come to Montana to gain control, not lose it.

The boys' squeals of laughter had her looking up from her churn. Quinn and Tommy were watching a frog peeking out of a hollowed-out stump. They were such good boys. Leaving them would break her heart.

"Abby, come help us catch the frog," Quinn shouted.

She pushed the plunger into the churn. It seemed all she did was work. For the first time since she'd arrived, she resented her chores. It had been so long since she'd had a bit of fun.

The clear creek waters glistened and beckoned. Abby glanced at her butter churn then back at the water, tempted beyond reason.

Excitement bubbled inside her. She quickly unlaced her shoes and tugged off her stockings. The boys laughed as she hiked up her skirts and stepped into the stream.

"Abby, you are getting wet," Quinn laughed.

She leaned down and splashed a handful of water onto the boy. "Now you are, too."

Quinn swiped the water droplets from his face then ran to the water's edge. "I thought we weren't supposed to get wet."

Abby shrugged. "Once in a while it's okay, Quinn."

"Pa says the bears stay close to the water."

Abby searched the tree line. "It's okay."

Tommy laughed at his brother as he ran past him into the water. He splashed Abby and then Quinn.

Not to be outdone, Quinn barreled in and started to kick up water. Abby laughed. The three played and time drifted. Soon water dripped from her hair.

Abby suddenly stopped. She felt the hair on the back of her neck rise.

She sensed Mr. Barrington's presence even before he spoke. Her back stiff, she looked down at her dress. She was drenched and the bodice fabric stuck to her like a second skin.

"Boys, you know better than to play in the creek. With that bear loose, there's no telling where it'll turn up."

Quinn looked up at Abby. "See? I told you."

She patted him on the shoulder. "It's my fault. Quinn did warn me."

Mr. Barrington reached out and hauled the boys out of the water. "It's time you went inside and changed into dry clothes."

"But Pa, we're playing," Tommy said.

Mr. Barrington nodded as he tried to brush the mud from the seat of Tommy's pants. "I can see that, but it's time to go inside." The steel in his voice left no room for argument. "Quinn, take your brother inside."

Quinn took his brother's hand. "Come on, Tommy."

Breathless, Abby hiked up her damp skirts and followed the barefooted boys out of the water. Dripping wet with muddied bare feet, she felt like a fool standing in front of Mr. Barrington. "There're sugar cookies on the stove after you've changed, boys. I'll get them for you.''

Mr. Barrington grabbed her arm, halting her escape. ''Boys, you go on ahead. Miss Abby will be there presently.''

''Can we have two cookies?'' Quinn said.

''Sure,'' Mr. Barrington replied.

When the boys were out of earshot, Abby tugged her arm free. ''They'll eat the whole jar if I'm not there.''

''Let 'em,'' he said. He held out his hand to her.

She considered ignoring him, and climbing out of the creek without help, and then decided she was being silly. She laid her hand in his. He closed his long callous-tipped fingers over her hand. Heat seeped up her arm as he hauled her out of the creek.

''You'd be smart to pay close attention while you're by the water,'' he said. His voice sounded gruffer. ''I found more tracks out on the range yesterday.''

Her stomach soured. ''More bear tracks?''

''I didn't want to tell you, but the other night when we were together—''

She shot him a look of warning, daring him to bring up what had happened between them in the barn.

He shoved out a frustrated breath. "*I* was talking about the bear tracks."

"I know," she said hastily.

He knew she was lying. "I tracked the bear the next morning but lost his trail half a mile from the ranch. There was no sign of the bear until today. I found more tracks."

"Are we in danger?"

He stood on the bank, his powerful legs braced apart. "We need to be extra careful."

She swiped a wet lock of hair off her face. The freedom and joy she'd just felt vanished. "We'll be more careful."

Abby lifted her damp skirts and tried to sidestep him. He moved, blocking her path. Slowly she lifted her gaze to his. The lines around his eyes and mouth looked deeper. Tension had tightened the muscles in his body. He looked ready for battle.

Suddenly, her whole body ached with sadness. "We made a mistake, Mr. Barrington, that's all. My leaving is going to correct it."

He stabbed his fingers through his hair. "You're right, we did make a mistake. *I made a mistake.*"

His admission added salt to Abby's wounds. He was sorry they'd made love.

Abby lifted her chin a notch. "I don't really blame you. I should have left town the minute I found out you didn't want a wife. I pushed when I should have retreated.''

He planted his hands on his hips. ''You've got spirit. I admire that about you.''

''Admire. Respect.'' Bitterness laced her words.

''Admiration and respect are good foundations.''

She searched his dark, clear eyes. ''What are you saying?''

''I don't want you to leave.''

''I will speak to Mrs. Clements about caring for the children.''

''This isn't just about caring for the children. I want us to build on the respect we have for each other.''

She shook her head sadly. ''When I first arrived I thought respect was all I was looking for in a husband. I didn't want love because it's too messy and painful. But the other night, my heart opened for the first time in a very long time. For a few brief moments I felt loved.'' Unshed tears tightened her throat. ''I've discovered that I want more from a husband, Mr. Barrington. I want love.''

He tightened and released his fingers. ''I don't know if I have that to give.''

Tears pooled in her eyes. ''I know. You've been saying from the start and I didn't listen. But I am now. I understand you can never love me.''

He lifted his hand to touch her arm, and then let it drop as if he feared touching her. "I still think we could manage well of it if you're willing, Abby."

"Manage well." She scraped a tear off her cheek. "Not the words of endearment I was looking for."

He swallowed. "I'm not a romantic man, Abby. Words are hard for me."

She could see that he was struggling and she couldn't watch this proud man suffer for what he didn't feel. "It's okay that you don't love me, Mr. Barrington. I know you are a fine man. You gave your heart to Elise and there's nothing else left to give. You don't have to marry me because of what happened."

"Many couples do well without love."

"You are right, but for the last few days I've been thinking about my parents. Theirs was a love match. What they had was special. And that's what I want."

His eyes narrowed a fraction as if he were trying to pry into her brain and analyze her thoughts. "Tell me about them."

She smiled. "You don't have to do this."

"What?"

"Make small talk. Like I said, it's okay you

don't love me. The other night was my fault as much as yours. Don't blame yourself.''

His lips flattened in frustration. ''I wouldn't be asking if I didn't want to know.''

She stared at him, trying to gauge his emotions. He stared at her with such intensity; she could almost imagine that he was interested. For reasons she couldn't explain, she started to talk.

''They met when my mother was working on a charity drive for the local parish. She was just out of the schoolroom. Mother didn't want to be at the church because her father had sent her as punishment. She'd had a tantrum because her last gown hadn't been made out of silk. Grandfather wanted to teach her humility.''

Her mother had told her this story a hundred times when she was a girl and she never got tired of hearing it. ''Father was a young parish assistant, just out of seminary. He, too, was working the clothing drive. He and Mother were assigned to work together.''

She glanced up at Mr. Barrington to see if he was really listening. To her amazement he was staring at her, listening closely. ''At first they hated each other. Mother hated missing her parties and she didn't like the young idealist minister who had grand ideas of opening a mission church for the

Indians. But Father was always teasing her, goading her into fights. 'No one could get under my skin better than Papa,' she used to say. Soon an attraction sparked and out of that grew love.

"My grandfather didn't approve of the marriage. In the end my parents eloped."

"What happened to them?"

"They had fifteen very happy years. They died in a cholera outbreak."

"That's when you went to live with your aunt and uncle?"

"Yes."

"That explains a lot."

"What do you mean?"

"My first impression of you was wrong. Dressed in that fancy dress of yours, you didn't look like you knew the business end of a stove."

She shook her head. "That *fancy* dress was a cast-off from my cousin."

"I've underestimated you. You are more than you seem. It's been a long time since I've come home to supper and a clean home. The boys have never been happier. You fit here."

Again no words of love. "I smooth people's lives. That what I've always done best."

"That's why you worked in the kitchens."

"After the trouble with Douglas and I realized

my uncle had every right to throw me out, I decided to make myself so useful that they'd never want to send me away. And it worked. Everyone in my uncle's social circle coveted my cooking skills. There was a pumpkin spice cake recipe that several fine ladies tried to buy from me.''

''You never sold it.''

''No. If I sold my recipes I could have been replaced.'' Looking at him made her heart ache. Traitorous tears filled her eyes. ''But I'm tired of just being useful. I want to know that if I got sick or I couldn't work there'd be someone to take care of *me*. I won't be just a convenience anymore.''

''I don't want you to leave.''

She sighed. ''I'll stay until the end of the summer as I first promised.''

He frowned, frustrated that he couldn't give her what she wanted.

''Thank you for trying, Mr. Barrington. But it's best I leave.''

Over the next couple of days, Matthias continued to arrive home before dinner. He played with the boys and tried to stay near Abby. He found all kinds of fool excuses to talk to her, whether it was the boys, the weather or cattle prices.

She was always polite and answered his questions, but she kept her answers short and her guard up. By the third day, he was running out of excuses to talk to her.

To Matthias's great relief, Holden arrived with his coach midafternoon on Friday. This time he carried three miners and a railroad executive. All the men ate their fill, and Abby was pleased to earn nearly five dollars for her meals. Reputation of her cooking was spreading like wildfire.

The men spent a good bit of time talking about beef and horses. The railroad was going to need both if it was going to bring a rail line up from Butte. With the railroad as a customer, Matthias would do more than break even this fall, he'd make one hell of a profit.

He should have been pleased by the development. After all, the lack of money had always been at the root of his worries. But even the promise of a hefty profit didn't soothe the tightness in his gut. He was losing Abby and he didn't know what to do.

Thirty minutes later, Matthias and Holden fastened the last of the buckles harnessing the horses to the coach.

"So how are things going with you and Abby?" Holden said as he rechecked the harness. "Abby seems extra quiet."

Matthias shoved his hands in his pocket. "Tense."

Holden shoved out a sigh. "Look, Matthias, I know we all sprung Miss Abby on you out of the blue. If things ain't working out between you two then I can take her back into town with me."

"No," he said, surprised at the force in his voice. "We just need a little more time to work things out."

Holden lifted an eyebrow. "So you're glad we sent for her?"

"She's one helluva complication."

Holden lifted an eyebrow. "A good complication or a bad one? I've had my life complicated by women before and I've got to say it wasn't all bad."

"It's not all bad."

"What are you gonna do?"

"Hell, I don't know. With Elise the love was there at first sight for both of us. Whatever is between Abby and me isn't clear-cut or easy."

Holden laughed. "Sometimes when you got to work for something you appreciate it more." His gaze drifted past Matthias to Abby who was talking to three very attentive miners. "But you better work fast. There are a lot of men who'd marry her in a heartbeat."

His gut coiled with hot jealousy as he watched a miner kiss her hand. "What the hell can I do?"

Holden scratched his chin. "For starters, I'd bring her into town for the Fourth of July picnic."

"Holden, I've got more work than I can shake a stick at. I can't spare two days."

Holden shrugged. "If you want to keep Abby you better consider it."

He didn't want to lose Abby. "What difference will a picnic make?"

Holden laid his hand on Matthias's shoulder. "Think about it. Women love social gatherings. Mrs. Clements and the other two women in the valley will be there. And you know how women like to talk. There'll be music, dancing and I bet Mrs. Clements would be happy to watch the boys for the night so you two could get a little privacy."

"If I tried to touch her right now, she'd likely brain me with a frying pan."

Holden laughed. "Which is exactly why you need to woo her, win her over."

"Woo my wife."

Holden shrugged. "Desperate times mean desperate measures."

"A picnic? Elise did like picnics."

"That's another thing. If you want to win Abby

over you're gonna have to stop comparing her to Elise.''

''Easier said than done.''

''How would you like it if every time you crawled into bed with Abby she was comparing you to another man?''

His jaw tightened just thinking about Abby with that damn Douglas. ''Point taken.''

''So we can count on you for the picnic?''

The idea was growing on him. ''The boys would sure like it.''

Holden groaned. ''This outing is about *Abby,* remember that.''

He watched Abby walk toward the house, her calico skirts billowing in the wind. There were a hundred reasons why he should love her.

However, he accepted the fact that the chances were slim. His heart had turned to stone, and he doubted anything would bring it back to life.

But for the first time in a very long time, he wanted to try.

Past seven that night, the fire crackled as Abby sat by the fire in a rocker mending a torn shirt that belonged to Mr. Barrington. The boys leafed through a two-year-old copy of *Harper's Monthly* magazine while Mr. Barrington reviewed his accounts.

The evening was painfully normal, and there were moments when it was easy to forget that she was leaving in six weeks.

"The horse roundup is going well. The herd is healthy and strong this year. I should make a fine profit when I take them to the railhead," Mr. Barrington said as he tossed another log on the fire.

The sound of his voice startled Abby. She looked up from her mending.

"I know you've been worried about that," she said.

"Abby," Quinn said.

Mr. Barrington glanced at his son, as if annoyed by the interruption, but he said nothing.

Quinn pointed to a pen-and-ink sketch in the magazine. "What's this?"

She glanced down over his shoulder to the picture. "That's a bicycle."

"What's a bicycle?"

"You sit on it and push those pedals with your feet. The wheels turn and you start moving. It's kind of like riding a horse."

"Does everybody in the city ride a bicycle?" the boy asked.

"Not so many people. It's hard to ride on the cobblestone streets."

"Have you ever ridden a bicycle?" Quinn said, looking up from the worn page.

She laid her darning in her lap. "No, but I saw one when the carnival came to town."

"I'd like to see a bicycle," he said. "Did you like living in the city?"

"Sometimes, I loved it. Sometimes it wasn't so fun."

"What did you like about it?" Mr. Barrington asked.

She glanced up at him, startled by his interest. "The theater. I would go once or twice a year. And the shops. In San Francisco, there are always ships coming in from the Orient. There are so many spices to choose from."

"Are there children there?" Quinn said.

She laughed. "Oh yes. Lots of children. Where I live they all go to the park in the morning to play in the grass. In the summer there is a merry-go-round."

"What's that?"

"It's a big wheel that has painted wooden horses on it and it turns round and round while music plays."

Tommy frowned. "Why would anyone want a wood horse?"

These children had lived their entire lives in wide-open spaces. Horses were a part of their lives. "It does seem rather silly doesn't it? But it can be fun."

She would have liked to have shown the boys San Francisco and take them to the merry-go-round and maybe buy them an ice cream. Then she caught herself. She'd be doing none of those things.

"What didn't you like about the city?" Mr. Barrington said.

Her gaze skidded to him. He still knelt by the fire. And though his voice had been casual she noted a tension in his shoulders.

"The crowds. The smells in the streets when the garbage is piling too high."

"And which do you like better, Montana or San Francisco?" Mr. Barrington asked.

"There's something to love about both." In truth she loved Montana best. "The city has a lot to offer but out here, there are not so many restrictions."

He nodded. "That's what drew me here. The freedom." He rose and leaned against the stone hearth. Tension seemed to wash over his body before he said, "There is going to be a picnic in town next week to celebrate the Fourth of July."

Before she could answer the boys looked up from their catalogue. "Can we go?"

Mr. Barrington stoked a poker into the glowing embers. "It's up to Abby. She'll be the one that'll have to make us the extra meals and get us packed."

The boys jumped to their feet. "Can we go? *Please*."

She wasn't sure what Mr. Barrington was up to. This ranch meant everything to him and time was as precious as gold. "Are you sure you can take the time? You're building that larger corral for the horses and you said you were behind on wood chopping."

His gaze stayed on the flames. "A family outing might be good for us."

Family. She wasn't going to do this. She wasn't going to let herself believe in things that weren't meant to be. "Giving up two days of work is not very practical, Mr. Barrington."

He frowned as if he'd not expected her to be so hesitant. Likely, he thought she'd jump at the chance. She wondered why she hadn't.

Quinn grabbed her hand. "Abby, please! I want to go into town."

"There's a pie baking contest," Mr. Barrington

said. "I'd be willing to bet you'd win hands down."

Tommy tugged on her skirt. *"Pleeeease."*

She stared into the little boy's eyes, so full of hope and wonder. "Mr. Barrington, you are backing me into a corner."

Mr. Barrington smiled, an occasion so rare, that when he did she found him irresistible. "I know."

Her stomach fluttered with tension. "We can go to the picnic, but be warned, Mr. Barrington, this picnic isn't going to change anything. My plans are set."

He rose and faced her. Like a warrior ready to do battle, his dark gaze burned into her. "So are mine."

Chapter Fourteen

Abby awoke in the middle of the night with cramps. It wasn't uncommon for her to have pain with her cycle but she'd not had real trouble in years. This month promised to be one of her worst.

Experience told her she needed something hot to drink. Groggy, she pushed herself off her pallet and climbed down her ladder. Since she'd arrived she'd always kept the fires in the stove burning to keep the chill off the cabin and make breakfast preparation less complicated. If she could just stoke the flames, she could make a cup of tea to soothe her discomfort.

Pressing her hand into her back she moved across the room, trying her best not to wake Mr. Barrington and the boys. She'd grown so accustomed to the cabin, she didn't need a light until she reached the kitchen. She lit a lantern, keeping the wick low so that the light wouldn't disturb the others. Soft buttery light hovered on the stovetop as she set the full kettle on the burner. It would be a good ten minutes before the water was hot enough for tea.

The pain in her back throbbed through to her stomach and shot down her legs. Of all the times to have trouble. Why couldn't her body have cooperated and waited until she'd left the ranch?

The creak of floorboards had her turning. Mr. Barrington stood in the kitchen. Since the bear's nocturnal visit, he'd taken to sleeping with his pants on and his guns within reach. She didn't need light to know dark stubble covered his square jaw.

"What's wrong?" he said his voice gruff with sleep.

She turned, the tea box in her hand. "I didn't mean to wake you."

"What's wrong?" he repeated. His gaze took in the kettle and the tea box.

"I just needed something hot to drink."

"It's not cold."

Embarrassment kept her silent.

He watched as she turned slowly and reached for a cup on the shelf above the stove. Her legs ached and she wanted nothing more than to crawl into bed.

He brushed her hand aside and took the cup from the shelf. "Sit down."

She just wanted to be alone. "Just go back to bed. I'm fine."

"Sit."

Too sore and miserable to argue, she sat down. Getting the weight off her legs felt good.

Mr. Barrington went to the front door and took the horseshoe that always hung there from its hook. He returned to the stove, moved the kettle to the back burner and laid the horseshoe on the hot front. "It should just take about five minutes to heat up, then I'll wrap it in a cloth."

Despite her best efforts, she slumped forward. "What are you doing?"

"Your stomach aches, doesn't it?"

She could feel the color flooding her cheeks. "I just wanted a cup of tea."

He shoved his fingers through his hair. "There's no cause for embarrassment. I understand what's happening."

Were the spaces between the floorboards wide enough for her to melt into? "I—I'm not embarrassed."

Amusement flickered in his eyes. "I've been married before, remember? I know what women go through each month."

She laid her forehead on her hand. She wanted to die. "I don't know what you're talking about."

He rolled his eyes and shook his head. "Get in bed with the boys. That bed is more comfortable than that pallet."

"No, I won't put you out of your bed."

"Get into the bed."

Too humiliated to quarrel, she crossed the room to the bed. Gingerly, she sat down, wincing as the mattress ropes creaked. She glanced over at the boys who both were in a deep sleep. Quinn was snoring. Tommy's mouth hung open.

Mr. Barrington dampened the tip of his finger and touched the horseshoe. Satisfied, he wrapped the horseshoe in a cloth as he moved to the side of the bed. "Go on, put your feet under the covers and then roll on your side with your back facing me."

Abby complied, grateful not to have to look him in the eye. The only person she'd ever discussed her monthly cycle with had been her mother and now to have Mr. Barrington ministering to her was almost too much to bear.

Gently, he laid the warm horseshoe against her back. And immediately, her muscles relaxed. "Oh my."

"Better?"

"Yes, much." She wasn't used to receiving help,

only giving it. "You should get some sleep. I'm feeling much better."

He didn't move. "I'll give it a few more minutes."

"No really, I can manage." She started to turn to face him.

"Is it always bad like this for you?"

The personal question stopped her dead in her tracks and she rolled back to where she was. Finally, she said, "No. It's usually not a problem."

"Well, if it ever is, get me up. I'll help you."

The heat seeped into her skin. Her cramps eased a fraction. "I'm not very good at taking help."

"I don't like it much, either, but I've learned it's a fact of life. Sometimes you need it."

Silence settled between them as he continued to press the horseshoe to her lower back.

Abby was grateful for the dim light. "You realize there won't be a baby now," he said softly.

"Yes."

A baby was the last thing she needed in her life now, but logic did little to soften her disappointment. Deep in her heart she'd hoped there would be a child to bind her and Mr. Barrington. Tears filled her eyes. She rolled toward him and took the horseshoe from him. "I wanted a baby."

He stared down at her, his face an unreadable

mask. Finally, he brushed the hair from her face and rose. "Get some sleep."

He picked up his guns, boots, shirt and lantern and started for the loft ladder.

"There's nothing binding you to me now," she said, her voice barely a whisper.

In the darkness, he paused. "Don't be so sure about that."

A week later the four of them were headed into town for the picnic. Abby sat next to Mr. Barrington on the buckboard seat while the boys sat on a blanket in the back.

Work, which had initially bound them, had kept Abby and Mr. Barrington apart while Mr. Barrington spent his days on the range doing his best to make up for the days he'd lose while in town. Whereas Abby, who was keenly aware that her time here was limited, worked twice as hard, as if somehow she could cram a life's worth of living into one week.

She had started a small vegetable garden by the house. She'd fretted over what she was going to bake for the picnic. She'd even found a pile of lumber in the barn that brought to mind her own dreams of staying and having an extra room added. The finely milled lumber had darkened with age—

clearly it had been in the barn for at least a year. Quinn had told her his pa had planned to build an extra room, but when their mother had died, he had put the project aside. Abby had shoved aside her thoughts of a new room and instead took extra care cleaning the boys' clothes and pressing a shirt for Mr. Barrington.

In the evenings both she and Mr. Barrington were so tired neither had the energy to speak, let alone be tempted by lovemaking.

Now as she sat next to him on the wagon, he was all she could think about. By rights, she should have been exhausted and grateful for the time to simply sit. But her muscles bunched each time his thigh grazed hers or he shifted in his seat. They'd hardly spoken since they'd started out this morning, but she was very aware of *him*—his strong hands clenched on the reins, his scent, and the way her breath quickened when his shoulder brushed hers. As the day had begun to heat up, he'd opened his work shirt. Sweat glistened from the thick mat of hair on his chest.

She imagined sliding her hand into the V-sloped opening of his shirt and touching the hair she knew felt coarse against her fingertips. She imagined herself removing his faded work shirt, kissing his skin, which tasted salty.

Abby ground her teeth. Why was she doing this to herself? Her thoughts weren't respectable or ladylike. What would it take for her to learn? She didn't belong with him.

The trip was painfully slow and it took until nearly lunchtime before she spotted the tips of the town buildings. Even from a distance she could see that the town had come alive. Wagons and horses dotted the horizon.

"How many more minutes?" Quinn said. It was a question he repeated each half hour.

Mr. Barrington pointed toward the town. "We are here, son."

The boys hopped up and looked around. The town's single street was filled with wagons and people.

"Where did all these people come from?" Abby said.

"From all over the valley. We've got about fifteen families here now."

A welcome banner tied between the mercantile and the saloon across the street flapped in the breeze. At the end of town there was a large table, covered with all sorts of dishes. Next to it a pig roasted on a spit.

Mr. Barrington tipped his hat to passersby who all openly stared at her. Uncomfortable with their scrutiny she tugged the edges of her jacket down. Everyone was used to seeing Elise at Mr. Barrington's side. Again, she was painfully aware that she didn't belong.

"They're not comparing you to Elise," he said in a low voice so only she could hear.

Startled by his dead-on accuracy, she sat a little straighter. "I wasn't thinking that."

"Yes you were." He sounded so damn sure of himself.

And she'd have argued with him if he weren't right. She was amazed how attuned he was to her thoughts. Finally, she relented. "People have to be wondering who I am."

He pulled the wagon to a stop in front of the mercantile and set the hand brake. He faced her. "They all know who you are. This valley is large but news travels fast."

"Still, they must miss Elise. She had to have had friends."

"Not really. Most people who live here today didn't live here five years ago when I arrived. Those that were here likely don't remember Elise. She was pregnant or sick most of the time. She only came into town twice when she lived in the valley."

"Oh."

"Miss Smyth!" Mrs. Clements's voice rang out

across the street. Carrying a basket full of bread she hurried across, dodging and waving to the other people. Breathless, she reached the wagon. "How are you doing? My heavens, you do look fit as a fiddle. Montana agrees with you."

Despite the turmoil, Abby was glad to see Mrs. Clements. She was a familiar face, and a woman to boot. "Thank you."

"Matthias, Mr. Stokes is here and he's looking to talk money for horseflesh."

Mr. Barrington nodded, tightening his hold on the reins. "I'll track him down."

Mrs. Clements chucked each of the boys under their chins. "Tommy and Quinn, I've a new batch of puppies. They're living under my front porch. If you are very quiet, the mama dog might let you pet them."

"Puppies!" the boys shouted.

In the distance, a brown-and-white dog sauntered out from under the porch. Her teats hung low and three puppies, no bigger than the palm of a hand, trailed after her.

"Can we go play with them?" Quinn shouted.

"Can we?" Tommy echoed.

Laughing, Mr. Barrington hopped down and rounded the wagon to Abby's side. He lifted each boy down. "You can go play with them, but mind that you don't stray far. I want you within shouting distance.''

The boys nodded. ''Yes, sir.''

''Well, go on then,'' he said, giving each an affectionate pat on the bottom before they ran toward the mercantile.

''I shall see you two in a minute,'' Mrs. Clements said. ''I've got to get these breads to the buffet table and there are so many friends who I've not seen in ages.'' The old woman scurried off.

''I do believe she is in her glory,'' Abby said, smiling.

''She does seem happiest when things are stirred up.'' Mr. Barrington held out his hands to Abby. ''Ready to meet your neighbors?''

She smoothed a curl off her face. ''They're not really my neighbors for long.''

His jaw tightened. ''They are for now and that's what matters.'' He wrapped his long fingers around her waist and lifted her to the ground. For an instant, he didn't release her. ''You smell like lavender.''

It pleased her that he'd noticed. ''I washed my hair yesterday.''

He captured a stray curl and held it between his fingers. ''Soft as down.''

Her mouth went dry. "Mr. Barrington, this isn't wise."

He didn't move. "What isn't?"

Her throat was suddenly as dry as dust. "Touching me. The last time we got too close we made a mistake."

Still, he didn't retreat. "When are you going to start calling me Matthias?"

The deep blue of his eyes tugged at her heart. If they weren't in the center of town, she'd have tumbled into his arms right now. Mentally, she gave herself a shake. "You are not going to seduce me, Mr. Barrington."

Even white teeth flashed as he grinned. "Care to make a wager on that?"

She lifted her nose a fraction. "It would not be fair to take your money when I know the outcome."

She took a step back and bumped into the wagon. He advanced a step. Her skirts swirled around his leg.

"No such thing as a sure thing, Abby. I learned that long ago."

An hour later, as Matthias leaned against a cottonwood tree, he was still pleased with himself. He'd spoken to Mr. Stokes and arranged for the man to travel out to the ranch to inspect his stock. In terms of the ranch, he couldn't have asked for a better day.

But his eyes right now were only on Abby. He watched Abby by the food table talking to Mrs. Clements and several other women. It was clear she was enjoying herself.

The women were laughing about something and Abby's clear bright laugh had him smiling. She looked so young when she smiled. Taller than the other women, she had full round breasts and a narrow waist.

He wanted to walk over to her now, take the pie from her hands and carry her to the closest bed. He could picture unbinding her long curls and stripping her neatly pressed calico down over her slender hips. The sunlight would glisten off her white breasts and the pink tips of her nipples.

He'd brought Abby to town so that he could woo her properly, but his courtship skills, which had never been refined to begin with, were rustier than an iron hinge left in the rain too long.

Holden, with a cold bottle of sarsaparilla in his hand, walked up. "Looks like Abby is fitting right in," he said.

Matthias stood straighter. "She has a gift for drawing people to her."

"Her cooking is making her famous. A couple of miners nearly got into a scuffle over the last piece of her pumpkin bread." Holden grinned. "Three have already asked for her hand in marriage."

Matthias ground his teeth and clenched his fingers. "She's not *that* single."

"Last I heard you two didn't say any vows."

Matthias was half tempted to wipe the smirk off the other man's face. "Yet."

"You better get on the stick. Single women just don't stay single long."

Matthias watched the rancher, Rawlings Collier was his name, walk up to Abby. He looked to be complimenting Abby on her cooking but Matthias knew food wasn't on the man's mind. The man was a known drinker and his livestock were poorly managed. "I think I'll ask her for a dance."

"'Fraid you're too late," Holden said, laughing. "Rawlings is guiding her out to the clearing where the others are dancing."

What the hell was he thinking bringing Abby to town? Matthias wondered. He watched as Collier danced with Abby. The man held her too damn close. He told himself he could be patient.

Abby's clear laughter rang out. She was trying to show the rancher a dance step. Collier was trampling all over her toes and Matthias didn't like the way his hand eased down Abby's back.

"Holden," Matthias said. "Is the minister in town today?"

"Sure is."

"Find him. I'll have a job for you before the day is out."

Holden chuckled. "Consider it done."

Mrs. Clements glided up to Matthias. "Our Abby looks like she's having a wonderful time. What's this, her third or fourth dance?"

"Fifth."

Mrs. Clements bit back a smile. "But who's counting, right?"

"Exactly."

"And have you seen the line of men over there waiting to dance with her?" Holden said.

Frowning, Matthias followed the direction of his gaze. "What!"

"Over there by the large cottonwood tree. I hear they are drawing straws so that it's fair."

He'd been so intent on watching Abby that he'd not noticed the collection of men by the tree. As Mrs. Clements had said, one held out his fist, which was filled with a handful of sticks. A rancher pulled out a stick and when he saw it was long, cheered.

The rancher turned the straw back in and walked to the back of a line now seven men deep.

That did it.

Matthias strode across the grassy field toward Abby. Collier had snaked his hand another couple of inches down her back. Dressed in faded denims and a clean gray work shirt buttoned up to his throat, he stood an inch shorter than Abby. He smelled of hair grease and bay rum.

Matthias bit back the murderous urge and managed a smile that looked a little like a snarl. "Abby, care to take a break?"

She glanced up at Matthias, her eyes a mixture of relief and worry. "That sounds lovely."

Collier held tight to Abby. "We just started dancing."

Matthias clamped a strong hand on Collier's shoulder. "You don't mind if the lady takes a break, do you?"

Collier frowned, stopping so suddenly he trampled on Abby's toe. "As a matter of fact I do mind."

Matthias squeezed as his gaze bore into the man.

Collier tried to wrestle his shoulder free but Matthias held tight. The man grimaced. "All right. But the next dance is mine."

Matthias grinned. "Sure, *pal*. But take your time. Have some punch. Maybe a cookie or two."

Collier glared at Matthias as he moved toward the saloon.

"You could have at least let the man finish his dance," Abby said.

Matthias took Abby's hand in his. The warmth of her skin felt good. "He was finished, he just didn't know it." He guided her toward the food table where he poured her a glass of water.

Her fingers brushed his as she took the cool glass. Grateful for the water, she drank it all down. "I've been craving water for the last hour but every time I went to get a cup someone else was asking me for a dance." She refilled her glass and drank more. "I've not danced like that in years and was having so much fun I didn't know how to say no."

He noted the rise and fall of her chest, the gentle curve of her neck, and the bead of perspiration on her forehead. These last few days, he'd worked harder than he ever had, hoping fatigue would dull his senses enough so that he didn't want to touch her. It hadn't worked. "You looked like you knew what you were doing out there."

"My parents loved music and dance. They both were quite good."

Damn, small talk had never been his strong suit, but he knew women liked it. And if he were going to win Abby he'd have to woo her properly. "How about we take a walk. I don't think you've had a proper tour of the town."

She glanced at the collection of eight buildings. Her eyes danced with amusement.

He laughed, pressing his hand into the small of her back. "All right, I'll admit it won't take long, but I thought you'd like to stretch your legs and get away from the line of dancers that are waiting for their turn with you."

She glanced over her shoulder. "There's a *line* of men waiting to dance with me?"

The glee in her voice grated. "Looks to be about a dozen at this point."

She grinned, satisfied. "My, my. I've never had a line of men waiting for me before. It's rather refreshing."

He guided her toward the mercantile. "Refreshing."

Her eyes twinkled with a bit of mischief. She really was enjoying herself. "I really shouldn't disappoint them. They seemed to be waiting so patiently."

If another man put his hands on her he'd break. "They can keep waiting. Right now you are all mine."

And he knew exactly what he wanted to do with her.

Chapter Fifteen

A warm glow spread over Abby as she stared up at Mr. Barrington. It would be so easy to love this prideful, strong man. She swallowed and pulled her hand out of his. "I really do think we better get back to the party."

His eyes narrowed. "What's the rush?" Frustration made his voice sound more like a growl.

"You are a dangerous man, Mr. Barrington."

His eyes narrowed. "And that's bad?"

She tipped her head back, willing her emotions to remain in check. "Very."

"Why?" His voice sounded angry, defensive.

"Because you are the very kind of man that I could love. You are honest, direct and there's no denying that you adore your children."

Her honesty disarmed him. "Then what's the problem? Stay with me."

"You'll break my heart," she whispered.

He rubbed his chin. "Abby, what the hell are you talking about?"

"Fool me once, shame on you. Fool me twice, shame on me."

He lifted an eyebrow. "You're talking again about that nitwit Douglas."

"At the time I loved him with my whole heart. I gave all of myself to a man who could never love me. I can't do that again."

He snorted. "You didn't give him everything, Abby. You were a virgin when we made love."

Made love. She liked the way he said that. "I wanted to sleep with him. I would have if we'd not been discovered."

"But you didn't. Because deep in your heart you knew it wasn't right, otherwise you'd have found a more private place to be with that twit. You're a smart woman. Your instincts are good."

"So my instincts are telling me that I should love you?"

"Exactly. Your instincts are just waiting for your brain to catch up."

She lifted her chin. He was so close to her right now she had only to lean forward and she could kiss him. "But your heart will always be with Elise." He frowned, ready to rebut, but she raised her hand to silence him. "Don't misunderstand. I will always admire that. You truly loved your wife. She was lucky to have had you love her. But no matter what my feelings, I fear that I would always be second to her."

He straightened his shoulders. "I will admit that a part of me died with her. But I'm not the same man I was when I met her." Scowling, he drew in a ragged breath. "I've learned there's more to marriage than love."

"Honest to a fault," she said grimly.

"Yes, I am. I'll never lie to you, Abby."

"I know."

She looked into his blue eyes. Right now he was as handsome as any man she'd ever seen. His black hair skimmed the tops of his open collar, which revealed dark chest hair that curled up from deeply tanned skin. His lips were set in a grim line, yet she remembered how soft they'd felt when pressed against her naked breasts. "I wish you could love me."

Before he could respond gunfire sounded. A scream echoed from the other side of town.

Mr. Barrington tensed instantly. "Stay here," he ordered.

"The boys!" Abby said.

"I'll get the boys. Stay."

Wild horses couldn't have kept her in her place.

He started running toward the party. And Abby was right behind him, running with her skirts hiked up. When they reached the picnic, her side ached from running and wisps of hair had fallen from her chignon.

A crowd had gathered into a semicircle. The fiddle player had stopped and no one was talking or laughing. Mothers kept their children close and the men stood angry and defiant. Most of them had left their guns in their wagons, in respect of the family gathering.

Abby searched for the boys but didn't see them anywhere. Fear ripped through her body and she ran along the ring of people looking for them. Finally, she found them on the front row, just feet from Collier. She ran to the boys. The instant they saw her they broke away and ran to her. She hugged them close. Fear jockeyed with relief. "Are you two all right?"

"Yes!" Quinn said. "He shot the mama dog."

Tommy burrowed his face in her bosom. Abby tightened her hold around his quaking body. All her men were safe and she doubted she'd ever been more grateful than now.

Abby took her first look at the shooter. It was

Collier. At his feet lay the mother dog that the boys had played with earlier.

Collier's crystal-blue eyes possessed a wild, dangerous look that made her skin itch. She remembered his sweaty hands on her body and how he had pulled her against him so that she could feel his arousal. She shuddered.

Holden, who'd been at the livery, ran toward the crowd, his hand on his gun. He pushed through the people to stand beside Mr. Barrington. All traces of the friendly man she'd known had vanished. He looked almost as savage as Mr. Barrington.

She glanced up at Mr. Barrington, but he wasn't looking at her or the boys. His gaze was trained on Collier.

"Best you leave," Mr. Barrington ordered.

"Miss Smyth owes me another dance."

"She's not dancing with you," Mr. Barrington growled.

Laughter cackled in Collier's throat as he stared at Mr. Barrington. "What claim do you have to her? None. But I'm willing to marry her here and now." To emphasize his point he fired into the air twice.

Mr. Barrington and Holden drew their guns so quickly Abby only saw the flash of sunlight glint off their barrels. Mr. Barrington fired. The bullet struck Collier's gun, knocking it from his hand.

A woman screamed. The crowd scooted back.

Abby flinched.

Collier's gaze darted between the two men. He inspected his shooting hand before he flexed his fingers slowly.

"Ain't I entitled to have a good time like the next guy?" Collier said. He snatched up a cookie from the table and took a bite out of it. Crumbs peppered the thick black stubble on his chin.

"Leave," Mr. Barrington said in an icy tone.

Abby sensed if there weren't women and children around, Mr. Barrington would have shot Collier.

Collier tossed the cookie on the ground. Instead of leaving, he leveled his gaze on Abby. "She owes me a dance."

Abby could feel her knees shaking even as she squared her shoulders. "I'll never dance with you, Mr. Collier."

Mr. Barrington stiffened, a sure sign he didn't want her speaking.

"Ain't I good enough for you, Miss High and Mighty?"

Abby opened her mouth to tell him just what she

thought of him, but Mr. Barrington shot her a look that told her to be quiet.

Chuckling, Collier dropped his gaze to the boys. "Is those your boys, Barrington? They sure are growing like weeds."

"Leave," Barrington growled.

Abby tugged the boys behind her skirts. "They are my boys and I'd thank you to look away from them. You're scaring them."

Quinn peeked around Abby's skirts. Collier scrunched up his face. He shouted, "Boo!"

The boy squeaked and buried his face in Abby's skirt.

Mr. Barrington cocked his gun. "Five more seconds and you die, Collier."

Collier held up his hands as if surrendering. "I was just making conversation." Carefully, he backed away and moved toward his horse, a black gelding with whip marks on his haunch. Collier swung his body up into the saddle. "They is your boys, isn't they Barrington. They got their ma's blue eyes. Elise was her name, wasn't it? My, but she was a pretty little thing." He let his gaze roam the length of Abby's body. "She ain't as pretty, but I wouldn't toss her out of my bed if she climbed into it."

Mr. Barrington fired his gun through the center

of Collier's hat. The hat fell off his head. A murmur of excitement rippled through the crowd.

Collier seemed unfazed. "You always was a good shot. But I'm better." He glanced down at his hat, poking his finger in the hole. "Maybe next time we'll get a chance to figure out who's best."

Mr. Barrington cocked his gun and this time aimed it at Collier's head.

Collier jabbed his spurs into his mount's side and rode off, kicking up dust on the food table as he left.

Only after Collier had cleared the end of town did the others begin to talk. Nervous laughter rippled over the crowd, but Mr. Barrington remained rigid. There was a feral edge about him that was both frightening and alluring. The beast barely reined in for society.

Mr. Barrington didn't relax his stance until Collier was out of sight.

Abby felt a ripple of excitement as she stared at Mr. Barrington's back. She'd never seen anyone so brave. Just the sight of him excited her beyond reason.

She let out a sigh. He didn't love her, likely never would. But she'd never wanted a man more than she wanted him.

* * *

Rage pumped through Matthias's veins as the crowd of townspeople smacked him on the back and thanked him. He'd worked hard these last six years to restrain the savage side of himself, but today it had nearly wrestled free of its chains.

When Collier had looked at Abby, he'd wanted to murder the bastard. And he'd have done just that if there'd not been so many children around to witness the violence.

Now that Collier had left, the homesteaders and townspeople started to talk. Their nervous chatter buzzed around his head. Several congratulated him but he was in no mood for niceties. Everyone quickly got the hint and started to back away from him.

Which suited him just fine.

Abby moved toward him with Tommy on her hip, Quinn holding her hand. Tommy had his head on her shoulder and was sucking his thumb. He noted how comfortably the boy fit on her very sumptuous hips. Her full lips were curved into a frown.

Need coursed in his veins and if he had his way he'd have dragged her to the first bed he could find and have her. They'd not see daylight for days.

What the hell was wrong with him? He was acting like an animal.

Matthias shoved a shaky hand through his hair. Life had taught him patience, and he desperately clung to each and every lesson he'd learned the hard way.

"I thought I told you to stay back. Stay out of sight." A portion of his pent-up rage tumbled out with the words.

Abby didn't flinch. "That man made me so angry I couldn't stay quiet."

His hand still on his gun, he fingered the smooth wood of the handle. "A woman out here needs to be careful. The polite rules of society don't apply here. His kind would think nothing of dragging you behind a building and—" He stopped when she cupped her hand over Tommy's ear. "You need to understand the dangers."

"I've an idea."

"You've no idea."

Fire flashed in her eyes and for a moment he thought she'd argue. "I'm not a schoolgirl, and I can assure you that even the city has its share of evil men."

A part of him hoped she would fight with him. He wanted to fight. Wanted to dispel the excess energy.

"Hey, Matthias," Holden said. "I'm going to take the dog out behind the barn."

Matthias tore his gaze from Abby. He looked down at the dog that lay in the dirt. What a waste.

"I'll take her," he said.

Just then the dog whimpered and Quinn squirmed his hand out of Abby's. "Abby, the dog isn't dead."

Tommy wiggled out of her arms and followed his brother.

Abby followed the boys. "Boys, stay back. The dog is injured and will bite if you get close."

Holden knelt next to the animal. "She's not doing too well."

"We don't want to hurt her," Quinn said.

Abby knelt next to the dog. Gently, she rubbed its head. The dog opened its eyes for a moment then closed them again. "But she doesn't know that. She only knows that she hurts and that she's scared."

"I'll take her away," Holden said, his voice grave. "No sense in letting it suffer."

Matthias nodded.

For the boys' sake, both men were careful not to say that they planned to shoot the animal to take it out of its misery.

Abby read the intent in his eyes. "Can't we try and save it?" she whispered.

Quinn looked up at his father, his eyes filled with tears. "Can't we save her?"

Matthias rubbed his hand on the dog's head. The dog lifted her head and licked his hand. Damn, but he felt helpless. "I don't know what to do for her, son."

Abby smoothed her hands over the dog's body. She lay still until Abby touched her back haunch. "Let me have a look at her."

Matthias would have argued if not for the look of hope in his sons' eyes. Feeling like he owed it to the boys to try, he gingerly lifted the dog and rolled it over. The dog yelped and growled but didn't snap.

Abby studied the dog's leg. "Her leg is broken. There's no doubt about that. But I don't see any other injuries. Collier shot at the dog but he may not have hit it."

"A broken leg is fixable."

Matthias tapped his finger against his knee. "I've set broken legs before."

"The dog will have to take it easy for a couple of months," Abby said. "Mrs. Clements has been feeding her and her pups scraps for weeks. She'll look after her."

Matthias nodded. He still had his doubts. This was a hard land and the weak didn't survive, but for now he was willing to give it a try. "Let's get her over to the livery. We can set the leg there and then find a quiet spot where she could rest.''

He lifted the dog again and headed toward the barn, with Abby and the boys on his heels. The inside of the barn was cool and shaded and he carried the dog to a soft pile of hay.

Abby found two large sticks outside the barn and hurried toward him. ''This should do.'' She knelt down and tore a strip of her petticoat off. ''And you can tie them with this.''

He accepted the strips. ''You boys stand back. I've got to set the dog's leg and she's not going to like it one bit.''

''Is it gonna hurt?'' Tommy said.

''Yes it is, son.''

Tommy popped his thumb in his mouth and held on to Abby's skirt. The boy had grown so attached to her.

Matthias ran his hand over the dog's leg. He could feel the break in the thigh. It felt clean, but there was just no telling. ''Abby, hold the dog's head.''

Without a word, she positioned herself at the dog's head and gently wrapped her hands around its snout. ''Ready.''

He spoke soothingly to the dog and then without warning snapped the bone in place. The dog jerked.

The boys screamed. Abby steady, never loosening her hold once.

Mathias quickly positioned the two wood sticks on the leg and tied them into place. He looked up at Abby. "Okay, let go."

She released the dog, who started growling as she sat up on her uninjured haunch. Then barking and growling more she hobbled over to a dark corner and sat down.

"What do we do now?" Quinn said.

Abby wiped her hands on her skirt. "For now, we'll just get her a bit of water and then we'll just leave her be. Later tonight, maybe we can bring her a bone to chew on."

"Is she gonna be okay, Abby?" Tommy said.

"I think she just might. She just needs time to heal now."

Tommy wrapped his arms around Abby's legs. "I love you."

Her heart clenched. Tears pooled in her eyes.

Feeling Mr. Barrington's gaze on her she looked up at him. She'd never seen a more handsome man.

"Marry me," he said quietly.

Chapter Sixteen

Abby looked up into Mr. Barrington's face. Emotion had deepened the lines around his mouth and eyes. "Are you sure, Mr. Barrington?"

"Very." His voice was strong, without hesitation.

Her breath stopped as her heart pounded in her chest. She glanced at the boys who stared up at her with expectant eyes. She truly wanted to say yes, but for the first time since she arrived, she was afraid.

Mr. Barrington took her hand in his, drawing her gaze back up to this. "We'll build a good life, Abby Smyth."

No words of love. But she'd not expected any. He was giving her all he could.

A thousand questions collided in her mind. Did

she really want this? Could she be the kind of wife he needed? Was she strong enough to live in Montana? She'd dearly wanted a sign from the heavens to confirm this would work. A crack of thunder. A gust of wind. But there was nothing. In the end, she realized marrying him now required that she take yet another leap of faith. "I think marriage is an excellent idea," she said softly.

He grinned and suddenly his face looked years younger. "Good." He picked up Quinn. "Let's find the minister."

Surprise tightened her muscles. "You want to get married now!"

He shrugged. "There's no such thing as long engagements out here. Besides, it'll be a few months before we get back to town and find a minister. I'm not waiting."

Giddiness collided with nervousness. They'd been at a stalemate since she arrived and now everything was changing so fast. "You're *really* certain about this?"

The deep intensity of his gaze made her feel as if she'd been caressed. "Very." He held out his hand to her.

Abby took his hand. "Let's find the minister, Mr. Barrington."

He squeezed her fingers. "Don't you think it's time you called me Matthias?"

She smiled. "Matthias."

Grunting his approval, he led her and the boys in search of the reverend.

The next few hours were some of the happiest in Abby's life. For the first time since her parents had died she felt as if she had found her place in the world. She'd never felt more at peace.

As she watched Matthias talking to Reverend Brown, she realized suddenly that this marriage wasn't simply a matter of convenience for her anymore. She loved Matthias Barrington with a power that shook her very core.

She understood and accepted now that he would never love her as he had Elise. But she felt in her heart that she had enough love for them both. She would work harder than ever to see that her new family thrived.

The wedding ceremony was simple. No fancy dresses, no special flowers or wedding bands. It was just her and Matthias standing side by side under the shade of a tall tree in front of the reverend with the boys and the townsfolk gathered around them.

Mrs. Clements dabbed a handkerchief to her eyes as she watched the two clasp hands. "I knew I had a knack for matching people up.'' The older woman leveled her gaze on Holden. ''It's a gift, pure and simple.''

Holden paled a fraction and took a step away from her.

Matthias cast Abby a sideways glance and winked. ''It will be good between us.''

No words of love, but she held on to the knowledge that her love would be strong enough for them both. ''It will be good.''

''Dearly beloved, we are gathered here today,'' Reverend Brown said.

The words drifted over her head as she stared at Matthias's profile. The thickening stubble already covered his square, tight jaw. His hair drifted over the top of his collar. Likely, when he'd married the first time he'd been clean-shaven and worn a suit.

''Do you, Abby Smyth, take Matthias Barrington to be your lawful husband in sickness and in health, till the grave separates you?''

''Yes,'' she whispered.

Matthias squeezed her hand, yet she noted his hands felt cold. He was nervous, she realized. Did he believe he was making a mistake?

''Do you, Matthias, take Abby,'' Reverend Brown said. ''To have and hold, in sickness and health, until death separates you?''

He lifted his chin a notch. "I do."

Abby took comfort that he'd not made the promise lightly.

"So by the powers given to me by the territory of Montana, I pronounce you married. Matthias, you can kiss your bride."

Matthias faced Abby then. He stared down at her, his eyes filled with a mixture of happiness and relief. Nervous for her first kiss as a married woman, she stared at his full lips and remembered that the last time she'd kissed him she could almost taste the fire in him. Her body tingled, eager for his touch.

Matthias bent his head and touched his lips to hers. It was meant to be a chaste kiss. Abby's body exploded with fierce desire. She wrapped her arms around his neck. He banded his arm around her waist and pulled her against his body. The kiss deepened and she was aware of the hoots and hollers of the crowd. Dear Lord, she was making a spectacle of herself. And she didn't care.

Matthias broke the kiss, glancing toward the crowd as if he were willing them to vanish. "Later, Mrs. Barrington. Later."

His rich husky voice was full of promise and Abby ached for what was to come.

The townspeople wouldn't let them slip away.

Weddings were too rare out here and the crowd intended to squeeze every bit of enjoyment out of it. The men toasted the couple. The women all had bits of advice for Abby.

Through it all, Abby waited with growing impatience for the time she and her husband could be alone. *Her husband.* She smiled each time she thought about the two words.

She looked up several times and found Matthias staring at her. The intensity of his gaze left her breathless and made her all the more impatient for the day to end.

Toward the end of the day, Abby slipped away to steal a quiet moment by a stand of cottonwoods near the creek. She knelt down and dabbed her handkerchief into the cool waters. Wringing it out, she pressed the cloth to her face as she heard people approach. Hating to give up her precious moments of privacy, she stayed hidden behind the cottonwoods, believing they'd soon leave.

"They look like a happy couple," the woman said.

The man grunted. "She's breathing. That's all he cares about right now."

"I'd say they are a love match," answered the woman.

"Love." Genuine laugher bubbled in the man's

chest. "Doreen, Barrington's a smart man. He ain't got no choice but to marry if he's going to keep his ranch. A wife is as essential to a man out here as a plow."

The woman snorted. "Well, Hyrum Winters, when you climb into bed tonight and are feeling lonely, don't be asking me for comfort. Drag your hide out to the barn and nestle up to that fancy new plow of yours." She flounced off.

"Now, Doreen..." Hyrum said, following her back to the party.

Abby's gut clenched as the rancher's stark words tumbled in her head. She rose slowly, tucking her damp handkerchief back into her cuff. Mr. Barrington...Matthias had married her because he cared about her and not out of economic necessity. Forcing herself not to dwell on the doubts that stalked her, she returned to the picnic.

Much later, when they'd accepted more advice than they'd ever need and tucked the boys into the wagon, they stood side by side under the night sky staring at the thousands of stars. They were so close, yet not touching.

Lord, how she loved this man.

She took his hand in hers. His fingers felt warm, so strong. He dropped his gaze to hers. His eyes gave no hint of his emotions.

"I promised myself that I would not do something but I have," she said.

He rubbed his thumb against her palm, but still he said nothing. Finally, he asked, "What's that?"

She pursed her lips. She had never been so afraid in her entire life. "I have fallen in love with you."

He brushed his knuckle against her soft cheek. "You are a fine woman, Abby Barrington. And I will do right by you."

Disappointment sliced through her. She'd wanted him to tell her that he loved her. She wanted him to banish the worries she'd harbored since the first. But Matthias wasn't the kind of man who made false promises.

She drew in a deep breath. "I know you can never love again. And truthfully, I have made peace with that."

He cupped her face in his rough hands. "Abby."

Her mind was rambling. "And it's not like we don't have love in our marriage. I do love you and well, you have a certain respect for me. So I think it's quite possible that our marriage will be successful."

He tipped her chin up to face him. He stroked the underside of her jaw. "I think we'll have a fine marriage." He leaned forward and kissed her on her lips. He tasted of salt and a hint of whiskey.

She ran her tongue over her lips. Lord but she loved touching him. She nestled close to him, wrapping her arms around him. Being in his arms felt so natural, as if they'd been together a lifetime.

He tightened his hold around her and she could feel his arousal pressing against her. "I promised myself the last time I touched you that I'd never do it again. No matter how tempted I was. I didn't want to take, when I couldn't give back."

She laid her cheek against his chest. His heart beat fast. "We are wed now."

"You deserve a proper wedding night in a real bed," he said gruffly.

She didn't care about fancy beds. If he'd said he'd loved her, the night would have been perfect. *Say you love me.* "A blanket under the stars suits me just fine."

He dipped his head and kissed her fully on the lips. She wanted him so much that she could barely breathe.

When he released her, she found that her knees were weak and that she could barely stand. He took her hand in his and scooped up several blankets from the back of the wagon.

They checked on the boys and confirmed that they were still sound asleep, and then hand in hand walked the twenty paces to the old oak tree. There the ground was smooth and covered with a thick coat of grass.

Matthias spread out the blanket as Abby watched. Her body tingled with anticipation. She tried to imagine what it would feel like to make love to him now that she was his wife. Would the passion still be the same?

He sat down on the blanket. He tugged off his boots and took off his gun belt and set them both by his right hand. He looked up at her. He patted the spot next to his. "Have a seat."

With the other bundled blanket in her arms, she took her place beside him. She stared up at him, suddenly unsure of what to do. This moment felt nothing like the wild abandon that had possessed them that night in the barn.

She supposed this was her cue to undress. Primly, she unlaced her shoes and set them on the ground beside her. She reached for her stockings.

Matthias's calloused fingers pushed her hands away. "Let me."

The smoke and heat in his voice had her looking up. A fire burned in his eyes that took her breath away. This night promised to be as erotic as the last they'd shared.

Abby moistened her lips as she set the blanket

aside and leaned back on her elbows. She held up her leg for him.

Slowly, Matthias's hand slid up her leg over her knee to the top of her stocking. He traced the band with his finger then slowly pulled the black stocking down over her slender leg. Her breathing grew shallow. Her heart raced.

Reaching for the buttons of her skirt, he deftly unfastened them. Eagerly she lifted her hips, so that he could pull her skirt over her hips. The cool evening air ruffled the soft fabric of her chemise.

She felt wicked, indecent.

Matthias's eyes glowed with dark passion as he straddled her hips and stared into her eyes. Quickly, he pulled his shirt off. Moonlight glistened on his muscled chest and flat belly covered with a mat of thick, dark hair.

He kissed her lips and then the hollow of her neck as he cupped her breasts.

When he lifted his head and reached for the buttons of her bodice, she slid her hand up his naked chest. His heartbeat was rapid and strong, his breathing shallow and quick. "Your heart is racing."

"I want you." He unfastened the tiny buttons that trailed down between her full breasts. He pushed open the folds of her calico bodice top and tugged it off her shoulders. The crests of her full breasts rose in white mounds over the top of her corset and thin chemise.

He kissed the top of each breast then moved back to her mouth. His tongue explored the soft folds of her lips.

She slipped her hands through his thick hair, savoring his taste and the feel of him.

In his arms, she felt as if all was perfect and right in the world. Her hands slid down his back to his buttocks then traveled around his belt and reached for the thick buckle. Her fingers fumbled with the buckle until it came loose. She unfastened the top buttons and eased her hand downward.

He hissed in a breath as if he had been scalded. "You're making me crazy."

She chuckled. "Good."

He stared down at her, the moonlight slashing across his rawboned face. He possessed intensity in his gaze that made her skin burn.

He covered her body with his and kissed her on her mouth. This time there was no holding back. They both began tugging and pulling at what remained of the other's clothes until they lay naked under the blanket.

He kissed her again, this time pushing his thigh

between her legs. She opened her legs wider, wanting to feel him inside of her.

Matthias kissed her naked breast, suckling it until it was a hardened peak. Abby swallowed, digging her fingers through his hair.

He pressed the tip of his erection at her feminine center. She grew moist and the desire inside of her nearly drove her mad. She lifted her hips, ready to accept all of him.

The passion stripped away all barriers and in one smooth thrust he pushed into her. Her moist hot body wrapped tightly around him.

"Abby." He whispered her name. His voice was so hoarse she barely recognized it. "Abby. Abby."

She understood the intent behind her muttered name. He was making love to *her*. There was no one else here but them.

She lifted her hips to accept all of him. And when he was hilt deep, he started to move his hips in a rhythmic movement that had her senses reeling.

When his fingers slid down to her moist center and touched her, her head dropped back against the grass. "Matthias!"

She wasn't sure what devilish thing he was doing to her but she loved it. Soon her body rose higher and higher until finally she couldn't hold back any longer. Her blood boiled hot, pumping through her veins.

Then, she tipped over an imaginary edge and her world exploded. She called out his name and dug her hands into his back. Every muscle in her body tensed as waves of sensations rushed over her.

He moved faster and faster until finally, his muscles bunched. Sweat glistening on his forehead, he growled her name and exploded inside her.

For several long moments, he lay on top of her, his head buried in the crook of her neck, his breathing rapid. Gently, she stroked her fingers through his hair as she savored every sensation.

If she lived to be one hundred, she'd never forget this moment.

Finally he rose up on his elbows and kissed her on the lips before he rolled on his side. He pulled her against his chest, spooning his body against her naked backside. He drew the blanket up over their warm bodies, and then cupped his hand around her breast.

Nestled against in his body, she was completely satisfied. For this moment everything was simply perfect. "I love you," she whispered.

He kissed her on the shoulder and hugged her closer against his body.

She held her breath as she lay on her side, waiting for him to speak some words of endearment.

But he said nothing.

Chapter Seventeen

"About time you two got here," she said. "It's past nine o'clock," Mrs. Clements said as she moved out from behind her store counter the next morning. "Lands, half the day is gone."

Matthias closed the door after Abby as the boys moved down the narrow center aisle. He was in too good a mood to be annoyed with Mrs. Clements's meddling. "We weren't in a rush." He squeezed Abby's hand, remembering how she'd moaned when he'd made love to her this morning before dawn.

Abby blushed as she ducked her head and pretended to look at a bolt of fabric.

The boys ran to a display of toys on the side of the counter. There was a set of jacks and a red ball.

Matthias couldn't help but grin. Last night had

been beyond anything he could have imagined. He'd never dreamed life could be so damn good again.

Mrs. Clements glared at them both, then grinned. She reached for a large jar filled with sugar sticks and pulled out two. Coming around the counter, she handed each boy a candy stick. "You two sit out front on the porch. I don't want sticky fingers near my new fabrics."

The boys' faces split into wide grins and they started for the door.

Abby stopped them before they could slip outside. She knelt in front of them and whispered something in their ears.

The boys turned and looked at Mrs. Clements. "Thank you."

The older woman winked. "You're welcome." When the boys were gone, Mrs. Clements planted her hands on her hips. "Well, I can see you two look like the cats that caught the canary."

Abby laughed. "We're heading back to the ranch and we wanted to say our goodbyes."

Mrs. Clements hugged her. "I wish you all the happiness in the world." She drew back and dabbed the corner of her apron to her eye. "I know you two will be very happy. Matthias, I hear Mr. Stokes plans to meet you at the railroad and inspect your horses.''

"He does in four weeks. I want to get to market so that I'm back before the first snowfall. I'd just as soon not leave home any longer than is necessary."

Abby smiled and took his hand in hers.

"We'll keep an eye out for Abby while you're gone. Holden will make regular stagecoach stops between now and then, so she'll have more company than she can shake a stick at."

Matthias nodded. "I appreciate that. After Collier's outburst yesterday, I don't like leaving her alone."

Mrs. Clements waved her hand. "He won't be trouble. Likely he's already sobered up and gotten back to his ranch."

"Let's hope so," he said. Collier did have a lot of work to do and any sane man would put aside grudges for the sake of his ranch. But Collier wasn't always sane.

The sound of the boys' voices drifted into the store.

"We better get going before they get into trouble," Abby said.

"Right. See you soon, Mrs. Clements."

Abby smiled. "Thank you again."

They turned and moved toward the door. Matthias's hand was on the door when Mrs. Clements called out. "Admit it, Matthias. You and Abby make a great team. And I knew best."

Matthias pressed his hand into Abby's back. He liked touching her. "You win, Mrs. Clements. You were right. We're a great team."

Satisfied, she folded her arms over her chest. "Ah, it's the sweetest sound in the world—a man admitting a woman is right."

A great team. Not a great marriage. Not a great love, but a team, as if they were horses or mules.

The words stuck in Abby's mind over the next few weeks, though she did her best to shake them.

During the days over the next weeks, work dominated their lives. Matthias herded his horses from the grasslands and corralled them at the ranch in preparation for the trip to the railhead. He worked from sunup to sundown and she rarely saw him during the day. Abby's days were just as busy. She not only had the boys and her usual chores, but their home was becoming a regular coach stop on Holden's route.

But the nights were different. They belonged to Abby and Matthias. After the boys crawled into their new bed in the loft, they would slip into their own bed. Their nights were filled with lovemaking.

She felt closest to Matthias during these quiet hours, when nestled against him, she would whisper her love for him. He would hug her close and kiss her on the cheek, but he never returned the sentiment. Still, with him so close she could almost convince herself that he loved her, too.

It was past two o'clock on a Sunday in August when Abby and the boys went into the barn to check on a newly acquired mare. Matthias had promised to be home early that day so that they could all share an early supper to celebrate her birthday. But he was already an hour overdue.

Abby hadn't started to worry yet. Matthias was working hard and likely had forgotten today was Sunday and that she'd planned a special meal. He had forgotten last week as well. And the week before.

The other weeks she'd shrugged off his tardiness. He had to work and she understood that. The stakes were high now and soon it would be make-or-break time for the ranch.

But this morning she'd asked him to make a special effort to be home on time. It was her birthday, she'd explained, and she wanted a special family dinner. Matthias had promised and kissed her goodbye and left.

Abby and the boys approached the stall. The mare, black with white spots, snorted.

"She doesn't look happy," Quinn said.

"She's just getting used to her new home," Abby said. She held out a handful of oats. The mare pawed at the ground but didn't approach. "It's best we leave her be."

"But I want to pet her," Tommy said.

Abby smoothed his wild hair flat. He and his brother both needed haircuts. "Maybe tomorrow. She needs a little more time."

"We should give her a name," Quinn said.

There was no sense naming the animals. Soon they'd leave with the others. "You two must be getting hungry."

"I am," Tommy said.

"When is Pa going to come home?"

She brushed his long bangs from his forehead. "Soon. Let's get you two fed."

"Can we have a piece of the cake you made?"

She'd hoarded eggs for a week so she'd have enough to make the cake. "Of course."

A half hour later the boys had eaten their fill of stew and each had eaten two pieces of cake. With only about a half hour of daylight left, she'd sent them out to play while she cleaned up.

Irritated that Matthias had forgotten her birthday,

she started to clear the table, stacking the dirty dishes in the sink and replacing Matthias's unused ones on the shelf.

She lifted her white tablecloth by the corners and took it to the doorstep where she gently shook it out. She was being silly, she knew, but for just a few hours she wanted Matthias to put her before the ranch.

Her face flushed, she carefully folded the linen cloth until it was a neat square. Her mother had served all her birthday dinners on this tablecloth. Abby had hoped to carry on the tradition, but it seemed Montana didn't allow such luxuries.

She heard Matthias's deep voice outside. He was home safe.

Ten minutes later after he'd unsaddled and watered his horse, Matthias, with a boy under each arm, walked toward the house. All three were grinning.

She wiped her hands on her apron, and managed a smile. "So what have you three been up to?"

"Nooothing," the boys said.

Matthias set the boys down and patted each on the bottom. "You two go wash up for supper."

"They've already eaten," Abby said. "I held supper as long as I could but they were hungry."

His gaze skimmed the table to the half-eaten

cake. "I've missed another supper. I'm sorry. But I got a good bit of work knocked out today."

Not just any supper. "The ranch comes first."

He walked to the counter and tore off a piece of bread from a half-eaten loaf. "The place looks great. You've been cleaning." He smiled, chuckling. "I've never known a woman to clean like you do."

"I just want everything to be perfect."

He brushed her cheek with his hand. "It is."

No it wasn't! She longed to turn her face into his chest and beg him to hug her. She needed reassurance now. She needed him to remember that this was her birthday. She needed him to love her.

Instead, she asked, "How is the herd looking?"

"Fat and ready to travel. The other homesteaders and I should be leaving in a couple of days as planned. If we don't run into any trouble we should be back by mid-September."

"Such a long time."

"I've always hated the time away from the ranch. But there's no getting around it." He kissed her on the tip of her nose. "But I'll be back before you know it." He pinched another piece of bread cooling on the kitchen table and popped it in his mouth.

"Wonderful."

His eyes narrowing, he tapped his long finger against his thigh. "What's wrong? You're not yourself."

She shrugged. "I suppose I'm just worried. I think about you on that trail."

He laid his hands on her shoulders. "I've driven the cattle and horses enough times. There's no cause for you to worry."

She ducked her eyes. "I'm being silly."

His eyes narrowed a fraction. "What's eating at you, Abby?"

"Today's my birthday," she said brightly.

Matthias shoved long fingers through his hair. "And I forgot."

"You did."

"Look, I am sorry. There's just so damn much work to be done."

"I know! The ranch always comes first."

Irritation flashed in his eyes. "For now, yes. That's the way it has to be."

Her stomach tightened into knots. "I never thought I could ever grow to hate this place, but I do now."

His face paled. He looked as if she'd ripped the heart out of him and instantly she regretted what she'd said.

"Matthias," she said, moving toward him. Lord, but she'd been churlish.

He shook his head. "There's nothing more to say now."

"Don't shut me out."

Before he could respond, Tommy and Quinn screamed. "Ma! Pa! The gate to the corral is open."

Their discussion forgotten, they ran outside. They found the boys standing close to the corral gate, which was wide open. The horses pranced on the far side of the corral.

Matthias reached for his gun, ready to shoot any horse that bolted toward the boys.

Abby hugged the boys. "Your father said to stay away from the corral."

"We found the gate open," Quinn said.

Matthias went for the gate. "Don't lie to me, boy. Which one of you opened the gate?"

Before the children could answer or Matthias could reach the gate, a shot rang out, spooking the horses inside the corral. Several of the horses reared and started to bolt toward the open gate as Abby reached the boys. She plastered their bodies against the gate, hers shielding the boys.

Matthias had only a split second to get out of the way of the charging horses. As he dove to the side he saw the flash of sunlight on a gun barrel. He hit the ground hard and rolled. That's when he saw Collier, on horseback, a hundred feet away. The lowlife fired another shot in the air, panicking the horses more. He started to ride off.

Collier had opened the gate.

A large black gelding rose up by Matthias. He rolled out of the way before the horse's hooves drove into the ground.

Energy snapped through his veins as he got to his feet and pulled his gun from his holster. In one fluid move, he raised his pistol and fired at Collier. He caught the rancher in the shoulder, but the man managed to stay mounted on his horse. He reined his horse around and took off.

Determined to hunt the bastard down and kill him, Matthias turned to grab the first horse he could. But thoughts of Collier vanished when he caught sight of Abby and the children. The scene he witnessed would haunt him for the rest of his days.

A black mare raced back toward Abby and the children. The horse reared, its hooves rising high above Abby's head. She cringed and covered Tommy and Quinn's bodies with her own. The children screamed as the horse's hoof came down hard on Abby's head.

* * *

When she woke up, she saw Matthias's face. Pinched with worry, the lines on his face looked deeper, as if he'd aged twenty years.

"Matthias," she said. "Where's Tommy and Quinn?"

Tears welled in her husband's eyes. "They're fine. You saved them." He swallowed as if struggling to regain control. "They are outside with Holden now."

"Holden is here?"

"He came to deliver news of Collier." His jaw tightened, released. "Holden found his body. Apparently, he'd stopped by the creek to nurse the bullet hole I put in him. He was mauled and killed by a bear."

She nodded, unable to summon sympathy for the man who'd endangered her boys. She tried to sit up, wincing at the pain that cracked through her skull. "My head."

Matthias pressed a dampened cloth to her head. "The horse's hoof clipped your head. You're lucky to be alive. Another inch and the horse would have crushed your skull."

She moistened her lips, and then tried again to sit up. Pain shot through her body. "I hurt all over."

Gently he touched her face with his hands. "Lie down. The last thing you need to be doing is sitting up."

Her mind felt foggy. "I've got a pie in the oven."

He smiled grimly. "The pie burned. Two days ago."

"Two days!"

"You've been out for two days."

She noticed then the thick stubble on his face. "But the horses…the stampede." The details were all so fuzzy. "Did you get the horses back?"

He took her hand in his. "Practical Abby." He kissed her hand. "No, I didn't get the horses. I've been worried sick about you."

"But you needed to sell the horses to the railroad. All that money."

He kissed her forehead gently. "The money doesn't matter. You do."

The emotion in his voice tore at her heart.

Tears burned her eyes. "I was being so silly about my birthday. I didn't mean what I said."

"I love you," he said. "I should have said it weeks ago."

"Matthias." To see this proud man so upset broke her heart. "You don't have to say what you don't mean. I understand you can give only what's in your heart.''

''I do mean it.'' He kissed her gently on the lips.

She closed her eyes, ashamed of her own actions. ''I shouldn't have overreacted.''

''Abby, look at me.''

She opened her eyes. She saw no traces of anger in Matthias's dark eyes, only pain and sadness.

''Abby, I made you a promise and I broke it.''

''You don't have to explain. You have worked so hard to make this place a success. And I said horrible things that I really didn't mean.''

''None of it matters without you,'' he said simply. ''And I should have told you that.''

''Matthias, please don't.'' She didn't want pity.

He cupped her face in his hands. ''I love you. These last two days and nights, I thought I might lose you.'' He swallowed. ''It would kill me if I lost you.''

Tears welled in her eyes as she stared up at him. ''Oh, Matthias, you will never lose me.''

''I love you, Abby Barrington.''

''And I love you, Matthias.''

Epilogue

May, 1880

Hilda Clements was bone-tired. But it was a good kind of tired.

She had to smile as she eased her backside into the chair by her writing table. The light from her lantern glowed onto a freshly written letter on cream-colored paper, a half-full inkwell and pen.

This year was going to be her store's most profitable. The railroad was bringing its rail line right past Crickhollow and soon the valley would be growing by leaps and bounds. Matthias and Abby Barrington's ranch had turned a fine profit last year. Matthias, with Holden's help, had rounded up his horses and sold them to the railroad. The Barrington horses were considered the best in the territory and he received top dollar for them. Abby's cooking had also turned their ranch into a prosperous stage-coach stop.

Two months ago they welcomed an addition to their family. Their daughter, Elizabeth, was one of the prettiest little babies she'd ever seen and there was no denying that Matthias, Quinn and Tommy doted on her.

Holden said that Matthias had nearly worried himself sick until the babe had safely arrived, but Abby had sailed through the delivery.

Hilda chuckled. She'd never seen a man more crazy in love with his wife than Matthias Barring-ton. Her matchmaking had turned out just fine. Fact, she doubted Matthias could have chosen a woman better himself.

Smiling, she dipped the nib of her pen into an inkwell.

Dear Rose—

I received your letter yesterday and enjoyed reading it very much. To answer your ques-tions, I run the stagecoach line in Crickhollow, Montana. I've lived here for eight years and my business is thriving. In the last year alone, I've added two more coaches and drivers to meet the growing demand. Crickhollow is a fine town, with a hotel, livery and a bustling mercantile. My life lacks only one thing—a wife, who'll share my life with me.

Rose, I'd be pleased to hear from you.

Yours truly,
Holden McGowan

Hilda stared at the signature at the bottom of the letter, satisfied that it looked very much like Holden's bold handwriting.

Holden was a good man who worked hard. Despite his success, he'd taken no time to move out of that shack he'd built behind the livery. He rarely had a proper meal and he'd grown too thin.

The truth was the man simply needed a wife, even if he wasn't smart enough to see that.

So, she'd taken matters into her own hands. She'd placed an ad in the *San Francisco Morning Chronicle*.

Hilda tapped her finger on the assortment of letters on her desk. She'd received three dozen letters from women interested in marrying Holden, but none had stood out like Rose O'Neil.

Yes, sir. Rose O'Neil and Holden would make a fine couple.

A fine couple indeed.

* * * * *

FALL IN LOVE WITH
FOUR HANDSOME HEROES
FROM HARLEQUIN HISTORICALS.

On sale May 2004

THE ENGAGEMENT
by Kate Bridges

Inspector Zack Bullock
North-West Mounted Police officer

HIGH COUNTRY HERO
by Lynna Banning

Cordell Lawson
Bounty hunter, loner

On sale June 2004

THE UNEXPECTED WIFE
by Mary Burton

Matthias Barrington
Widowed ranch owner

THE COURTING OF WIDOW SHAW
by Charlene Sands

Steven Harding
Nevada rancher

Visit us at www.eHarlequin.com

HARLEQUIN HISTORICALS®

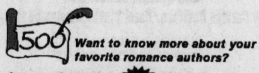

FALL IN LOVE WITH
THESE HANDSOME HEROES
FROM HARLEQUIN HISTORICALS

On sale September 2004

THE PROPOSITION
by Kate Bridges

Sergeant Major Travis Reid
Honorable Mountie of the Northwest

WHIRLWIND WEDDING
by Debra Cowan

Jericho Blue
Texas Ranger out for outlaws

On sale October 2004

ONE STARRY CHRISTMAS
by Carolyn Davidson/Carol Finch/Carolyn Banning

Three heart-stopping heroes
for your Christmas stocking!

THE ONE MONTH MARRIAGE
by Judith Stacy

Brandon Sayer
Businessman with a mission

www.eHarlequin.com

HARLEQUIN HISTORICALS®

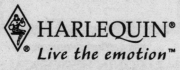

Savor these stirring tales of romance with Harlequin Historicals

On sale May 2004

THE LAST CHAMPION by Deborah Hale

Once betrothed, then torn apart by civil war, will Dominie de Montford put aside her pride and seek out Armand Flambard's help to save her estate from a vicious outlaw baron?

THE DUKE'S MISTRESS by Ann Elizabeth Cree

Years ago Lady Isabelle Milborne had participated in her late husband's wager, which had ruined Justin, the Duke of Westmore. And now the duke will stop at nothing to see justice served.

On sale June 2004

THE COUNTESS BRIDE by Terri Brisbin

A young count must marry a highborn lady in order to inherit his lands. But a poor young woman with a mysterious past is the only one he truly desires....

A POOR RELATION by Joanna Maitland

Desperate to avoid fortune hunters, Miss Isabella Winstanley poses as a penniless chaperone. But will she allow herself to be ensnared by the dashing Baron Amburley?

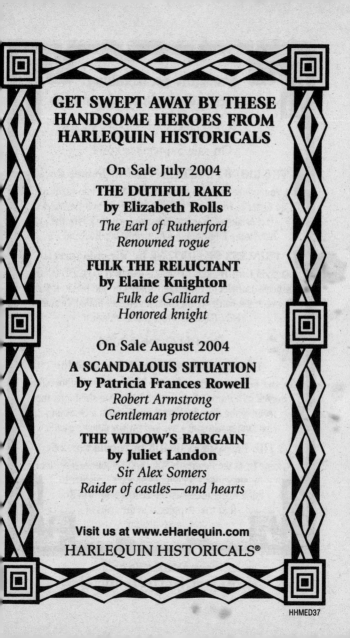